S0-CFU-735

Stitch in Time

L.J. Mainville Jr.

AuthorHouse™
1663 Liberty Drive
Bloomington, IN 47403
www.authorhouse.com
Phone: 1-800-839-8640

First published by AuthorHouse 11/05/2009

ISBN: 978-1-4490-3134-3 (e)
ISBN: 978-1-4490-3133-6 (sc)

Library of Congress Control Number: 2009911409

Printed in the United States of America
Bloomington, Indiana

This book is printed on acid-free paper.

Dedicated to my Parents
Leo and Geri
Without whom
these stories could never be told.

FORWARD

I had to be around 10 or 11 years old when I got my first Model car to build. It was a birth-day present from my God Mother; I don't know what made her think I was the Model building type but she was always getting me stuff like that. One year she got me a wood burning kit but I used it to melt crayons and my sister's Barbie dolls.

"That's a Model T Ford". My father said as I pushed the gift aside. I was hoping to get the Evel Knievel Motorcycle guy, so I reached for the next present that looked to be the right size. "If you're not gonna build it, I'll take it." My dad said as he picked up the model. "It's not like you'll know what you're doing anyway."

I'll never forget the embarrassment I felt as he said that to me. The way he snickered at me as he said it and then elbowed the joke to my Uncle made me furious. I reach out like a bolt of lightening and snatched it out of his hands as I proclaimed, "I will so know what to do with it!"

Later that night, after taking my shower, I went up to my room and sat at my desk and started to work on the model, just to prove my father wrong. I did my best to follow the directions and glued all the car parts together. I built the engine as the instructions suggested and after a few hours of breathing Model Glue, and reading fine print instructions printed on rice paper, I sat back and admired my work. However, the wheels were a bit crooked and the windshield was stained with a thumb print in model glue. It didn't look quite like the picture on the box, so I thought I could jazz it up by painting race stripes on the side "That should liven it up a bit" I thought to myself. However, my hand wasn't as steady as I needed it to be and the thick oil based paint was clumping up. I grabbed some toilet tissue and tried to clean off the paint, but it was sticky and the toilet paper started breaking apart and sticking to the paint and excess glue that was on the car. Before I knew it, I had clumps of red and orange paint balls stuck to my fingers and hands and all over the car. Looking around my room and thinking quickly, I pulled the eraser off of a pencil and tried to use the medal band as a type of make-shift paint scraper, but my efforts were futile.

Had I just left the car as it was, I may have gotten an 'Atta Boy' from my father. But after trying to fix it up I only made matters worse. I pulled out my trash can and dropped the tissue covered car into it along with the box, instructions and paints. I never built a model ever again.

Such is the story of my life. Whenever I try to make things better, I usually end up with a toilet tissue covered model car that is worthless. If only I can learn to NOT try and make things better than they already are.

CHAPTER ONE

As he rounded the corner from Front Street to Cataract Street, he looked up from the pavement and gazed at the block of row homes that lined the street before him. Odd numbered building on the right hand side of the street and even numbered building on the left. Immediately he smiled as fond memories of his youth filled his heart and mind. He took a few paces and stopped as he suddenly remembered something. He spun to the right and gazed up at the three story brick building where his grandmother had once lived. The building was painted an odd green color now, but the faded red brick was still showing where the paint was flaking away from the two hundred year old bricks. The building sat on the corner of the street with the Mohawk River behind it and the long view of 'Front Street' before it. There were old curtains in the second story window, so he couldn't make out if anyone was actually living there or not. He crossed the street so he could get a better view of the second floor window when suddenly his mind placed an image of his grandmother leaning out of the window and yelling at the neighborhood kids as they ran down the street laughing loudly. Stitch's first memories were right at this building where his Grandmother lived for so many years. It gave him an eerie feeling to be standing in front of it. He smiled as he recalled his grandmother's reddish gray hair up in curlers and her over weight body covered with sheer linen that she made into a dress. She was a very large woman and had difficulty with normal fitting clothes, so she would have to hand make her own clothes to fit her. ***This is probably what all the neighborhood kids were laughing at.*** He thought to himself with a guilty smile. He walked up the street a little further and was saddened by the fact that there were no children playing on the street. When he had lived here as a kid, all the neighborhood children would play in the street, or sit on the stoop where they would chew gum and see how far they could spit. There was never a time when there were no kids on the street; not even at night. Now his old neighborhood seemed desolate and barren. He almost expected tumbleweeds to come rolling down the middle of the road. "I guess the old saying is true". He said aloud. "You never can go back home." Something his cousin, Vince had told him shortly before Stitch was to leave for the Navy. Stitch had mentioned how he couldn't wait to return home to see his friends and show off his Navy uniform; but his cousin, who had been in the Navy and came back after boot-camp, told him it's never the same again. 'It's never *home* again'. He found this to be quite true as he walked up the barren, childless street.

Stitch stopped in front of another building that had two porches, or 'stoops' in front of it. The first stoop belonged to building number two and the second stoop was number four. Stitch's Aunt Terri and Uncle Danny lived in building number two when he was a little kid. He loved them dearly, and missed having them around. Stitch remembered his Uncle Danny was a magician and a professional clown and he would always do magic tricks for Stitch or tell jokes. Stitch had always wanted to grow up and be just like his uncle. He wanted to make people laugh, and share in their joy. However, he wasn't too keen on the idea of clown make up, so he thought about doing something along the lines of Stand-Up Comedy or maybe a famous television star. He also thought about becoming a radio disc jockey since they like to make people laugh too. When Stitch was a kid he listened to the morning D.J. on an AM radio station and thought he was the funniest guy he'd ever heard, aside from his Uncle Danny.

As Stitch stood in front of the row homes, he tried to remember who lived on the first floor, under his aunt and uncle, but couldn't remember who it was; so he moved along to the next stoop. Stitch had lived in building number four, which was next door and as he stood there, he actually closed my eyes and remembered the fun and happy times he had while living there; and also the not-so happy times. As he reminisced, he felt a tap on his arm, which jolted him back to reality. He looked to his left and spied a young boy of 10 or 11 years looking up at him curiously. "Are you all right, mister?" His one eye was squinting out the sun, which was shining brightly off Stitch's shaven head.

Stitch smiled as he answered, "I used to live here when I was your age." He pointed up at the second floor windows. The boy looked up and Stitch pointed to a set of third floor windows that were directly under the eave of the roof. They were quite short, around eighteen inches high and only two feet wide. "Those windows were my bedroom" Stitch said, guiding the boy to look up.

"That's where I sleep." The boy replied, almost excited by the news. Just then the front hall door opened and an attractive woman, who looked a little younger than Stitch, stepped out; apparently looking for the boy who was speaking with Stitch.

"Steven!" She said with some nervousness in her voice. "What have I told you about speaking to strangers?"

"But..." the boy started. However, the woman would not let him finish as she gestured to him to get up on the stoop. Stitch began to feel guilty as he realized this wasn't the same street where he had spent his childhood, at least not the way it used to be. ***Things back then were very different from the way they are now***. Stitch thought to himself.

"I'm sorry, Ma'am." Stitch said, making sure not to step in her direction. He didn't want to come across as threatening so he took a step back and placed his arms behind his back. "I was just telling your son that I used to live here when I was his age and he was kind enough to humor me as I..."

"Nephew". She said, cutting his sentence short. There was no smile on her face or in her voice. She was very serious and wanted to make sure that Stitch *knew* she was serious.

"Excuse me?" Stitch was confused as to what she was referring to.

"He's not my son, he's my nephew." She reiterated as she stood atop the highest step with her arms crossed over her chest. Despite how threatening she wanted to look, Stitch found her fascinating with her brown hair highlighted and up in a ponytail. She looked down at him as if she would pounce if he moved an inch so he simply nodded acknowledgment.

"Your nephew is a polite child."Stitch said as tried to ease the situation and assure her that he wasn't a threat. "It's just that I haven't been back here in quite some time and thought it would be nice to visit my old neighborhood, although I must admit", he smiled as he was about to make a light joke. "I didn't think I'd be coming back home for the last time." All he could do was smile and surprisingly she returned his smile. "You see, if you kill me, I won't ever be coming back..." His little joke bombed, but if he learned anything from watching late night television, if you try to explain a bad joke, the explanation can be funny; and he did his best to recover. Regardless of how silly his joke was her smile allowed him to feel comfortable enough to bring his hands out from behind his back and take a step closer. He extended his hand to the woman and introduced himself. "I'm Stitch LeRue." He said as he stared into her eyes. Just then, she seemed to perk up and she stepped down one step and shook his hand as she commented on his family name.

"My landlord's name is LeRue." She said.

"That would be my father's brother, Billy."

"No." She replied and then thought for a moment before responding. "It's Paul, I think."

Dad's baby brother. Stitch thought to himself. "Paulie is one of my other uncles."

"Really?" The woman looked surprised. "Because he doesn't look *that* old." She said before realizing just how it sounded, "I mean.. you know.. to be *your* uncle..."

Stitch could have taken her comment as an insult, but instead he smiled as he understood what she meant.

"My grandparents had 17 children and Paulie is the baby of the bunch." He said trying to assure her she had nothing to feel embarrassed about. "It's true!" Stitch exclaimed as he noticed a look of disbelief in her eyes. "My grandparents and their kids were known on this street as the *LeRue Clan*". Stitch pointed to the old green brick house on the corner as he spoke some more. "My mother's mother, who was kinda mean, used to call my dad's parents,

Jack Rabbits". Stitch found the woman to be very attractive as she covered her mouth and giggled. He told her how his uncle was just a few years older than he and how awkward it was to have to call him 'Uncle', but Stitch's father told him it was a sign of respect. As a child, he used to wonder, ***why the hell do I need to respect that little turd***? But he did, otherwise, Stitch's father would have kicked his ass up and down Cataract Street.

"That's a lot of children to have." She said.

"They grew up in that apartment, right there." Stitch said as he pointed to number two, the apartment where his Aunt Teri and Uncle Danny had once lived. "And my mother grew up just across the street, in building number one." He gestured his thumb over his shoulder to the badly painted brick house but never took his eyes off her. There was something captivating about her, but that wasn't why he couldn't stop looking at her. She looked familiar but he couldn't place her face. He let it go and thought if he did know her; it would eventually come back to him.

Stitch suddenly felt awkward and thought she might have tolerated enough of him so he excuse himself. "Well, I've taken enough of your time." he said as an excuse. "Thank you and be sure to thank your nephew for me too". And just as he started to leave...

"Wait." She said, stopping him in his tracks. "Would you like to come up and see the apartment?"

He tried to contain the smile on his face but did a poor job of it. He really did want to see the place since it had been so many years since he'd been there. Part of him didn't think he should accept the offer, but he pushed that paranoid little geek back into the pit of his stomach and proudly accepted her offer. "I would love to come up and see it." He said. "As long as it won't be an imposition on you or your nephew."

"If it were, I wouldn't have invited you." Her tone was sincere, yet with a hint of sarcasm. It made Stitch smile to know there was someone else who shared his style of humor.

As Stitch climbed up the four concrete steps of the front stoop, he thought how long it had been since he'd actually stood there. He smiled as he realized how small they really were compared to how big they seemed when he was just nine-years-old. As he passed through the wooden hall door, he made the same realization; that it wasn't as large as he'd remembered it to be. When he was a child, it seemed gigantic, green and assuming. He took notice of the floorboards in the hallway as they were the same, old wooden planks that were there as he grew up. Probably the same planks that were used when the building was first built back in the late 1800's. This small, upstate New York town was built on the edge of the Mohawk River, just at the foot of waterfalls. The falls powered the industrial mills, just a few blocks down the main road. Back before the turn of the 20th century, those mills were responsible for manufacturing textiles, clothing, and metals for the entire country. The falls not only generated the power to run the mills, but also served as a way to ship the manufactured goods through the Erie Canal, across New York State and to the rest of the country via the Great Lakes. All the homes built on his street were built to house the mill workers way back when. Every single building still had all the original bricks and boards and even gaslight piping in the hallways. The New York historical society said it would be a crime to destroy or change these buildings and they were left in their original condition. However, Stitch was still surprised at how well his Uncle was able to keep the buildings in such a livable fashion without upsetting the historical society. Even though the walls were painted, you could still see the print of the original wallpaper beneath. Overhead, the ceiling was covered with a tin cast that had artsy décor along the borders. Suddenly, Stitch remembered the ceiling in the living room and how the borders used to look like Easter eggs lining the walls. The kind woman gestured up the stairs and Stitch followed. As he took his first step he reached out and touched the banister and suddenly it's cool, smooth, wooden surface felt vividly familiar to him and instantly he was nine years old, walking up the steps of the front hall once again...

June 15th, 1973

He crept slowly up the stairs, being careful of the squeaky steps. The fourth from the bottom, two up from that one and then the next one, but stay to the right side of it... Stitch did his best to sneak in as quietly as possible. It was late and his father told him to be home before the streetlights came on, but it was way past that now. Stitch had gone up the road to see a girl he had a crush on. Her name was Celine Tyler, and to him she was the most beautiful girl in the entire school. While riding bikes with his cousin one day, he had seen her playing in her back yard and he couldn't believe how close she lived to him. With school almost over for the summer, he wanted to make sure he could see more and more of her. She was one of the reasons he enjoyed going to school so much, and the main reason he dreaded summer. But now that he knew she lived close by, he could enjoy the summer just like everyone else. On this particular day, Stitch and Celine swung on her swing while her mother brought cookies and lemon-aid to them. Stitch was positive that he was feeling genuine love and he didn't want to stop feeling it. He might have only been nine-years-old, but no one could tell him different. As they swung on the swings and talked about their teachers, while eating peanut butter cookies, Stitch noticed the street lights had come on. He knew he needed to be home by the time the lights came on and he realized he was late in doing so, but he had to stay for a just a little while longer. He may have only been nine years old, but this was the best day of his life and he didn't want it to end. However, Celine's mother called her in and told her it was time to take a bath. Celine jumped off the swing and gave Stitch a hug. "Thanks for playing with me today, Stitch." She said before running to her mother who was still waiting for her at the back door. She stopped and waved to him before her mother instructed her to hurry into the bath. Stitch just stood in the middle of Celine's back yard, frozen in like a statue with a cookie in one hand and a half glass of lemon-aid in the other. His slack jaw let bits of cookie crumbs to fall to the ground as he couldn't believe that Celine Tyler just hugged him. The back porch light of Celine's house went dark and Stitch realized he must be more than late and he immediately placed the glass of lemon-aid on the picnic table and started running as fast as he could. He jumped on his bike and began peddling down North Mohawk Street, past St. Patrick's Church then turned left onto School Street and down the back alley. He quickly opened up the gate to his back yard and dragged his bike into the shed before he tried the back door, but it was locked. *OH CRAP!* Stitch thought as he ran out the back gate and around the long stretch of row homes to the front. He ran up the steps of his stoop and pushed open the large, green front hall door and froze at the bottom of the stairs. He had to be very quiet getting up to his room. He knew the kitchen door at the top of the stairs would be closed and the living room door was never used, so he should be able to sneak up the next set of stairs into his room and pretend like he'd been there all night long. However, the stairs squealed worse than his sister Caitlin and he needed to take caution as he ascended them. When he reached the top of the first flight of stairs, he glanced at the kitchen door and could see a silhouette of his father through the window curtain. Stitch froze in his tracks as he knew his father could hear the slightest move.

"Caitlin." His father called from the kitchen to the living room.

"What?" Caitlin yelled back from the living room. Yelling was something that the LeRue family did often. No one really got up and walked from one room to the next in order to say something, they just screamed from one room to the next and at times, it drove Stitch crazy. However, he couldn't say that he wasn't guilty of it himself from time to time.

"Go upstairs and tell your brother to come down here right now."

Stitch could hardly believe it. His plan had worked and he didn't even have to do anything. He rubbed his eyes to make them look like he had been reading all evening, and then walked through the kitchen door. "There you are." His father said, turning around from the counter to face him. "What the hell have you been doing up there all this time?"

"Homework." Stitch replied with a fake groggy sound to his voice. He had mastered the art of using his throat to sound tired. It worked every time. The fact of the matter was he *did* have homework, but it had been sitting on his desk the entire night while he was swinging on Celine's swing and gnawing on cookies and playing googly eyes with the pretty girl. But there was no way he was going to let Leon know that. Stitch knew he had all weekend to make sure it was finished for Monday morning.

"You forgot to take out the friggin' garbage." His father said, while pouring a cup of coffee. Stitch winced in disgust as he couldn't stand the smell of coffee; not even coffee ice cream. The smell of it made him sick to his stomach. "If I told you once, I told you a thousand times! *Take out the garbage after dinner!*" Stitch knew he was supposed to take out the garbage, but he was in such a hurry to get to Celine's house, he thought he could get home early enough to do it without his father realizing. He just stood there, staring up at his dad trying to come up with a reason for not taking it out. His father was tall and thin and in his late thirties. His hair was black as coal and his face always sported a five o'clock shadow, no matter how often he shaved. He was wearing khaki trousers and a khaki shirt with work boots just like any other day. Leon worked in a metal shop at the mills and it seemed as though he was always wearing his work clothes. When Leon couldn't get a response out of Stitch, he reached out and grabbed the boy by the collar of his T-Shirt and pulled him close to his face while speaking through clenched dentures. "I'm not raising you to be a lazy, good-for-nothing slob! Do you understand me"? The pungent smell of Maxwell House and non-dairy creamer mixed with cigarette breath made Stitch's stomach do flip-flops. The fact that his father had pulled him to just an inch or two from his face made it all the worse. He turned his face away from his father's, but this only made Leon angrier. Stitch was relieved when his dad pushed him back towards the garbage bag that was sitting by the kitchen door. He stumbled and fell onto the bag before hitting against the kitchen stove. "Now get that fuckin' bag down to the shed or I'm gonna knock you into next week!" Leon always had a way with words when he got angry. Telling his son things like, "You're so fuckin' lazy you stink" or "You're so goddamned stupid, you'll never amount to anything!" were just some of the terms of endearment that he used on his son. But it didn't really phase Stitch all that much, he knew it was just words and Leon only said those things when he was upset.

After picking himself up out of the trash Stitch lugged the overweight bag of trash down the back stairs. With one hand pulling the at the bag, he used the other hand to pull at his t-shirt to get rid of the wrinkles that his father created and muttered something about how being the oldest child sucked more than anything.

"I HEARD THAT!" Leon yelled from the kitchen. Stitch froze for a moment, amazed at how his father could hear a whisper through the walls and then resumed taking out the trash.

With the trash taken out and the day at its end, Stitch was sent to the bathroom to take a shower. Stitch hated showering, but the apartment didn't have a bathtub because the bathroom was too small and could only house a hanging porcelain sink, a shower stall and a toilet. Each time Stitch would take a shower; he would have to play with the knobs and he ended up either scalding himself or freezing himself to the point where he had to call for help. Leon would always burst in to the bathroom and start yelling about how the shower was set *just right* and that he didn't want Stitch to play with the knobs.

"I can't help it." Stitch would say. "The water was getting cold!"

"Don't bullshit me!" Leon would retaliate. "The Hot Water tank isn't that small you know!" Stitch would try to explain that the water was getting colder and he was trying to set it back to warm, but his father wouldn't hear it. Instead, he would yell at Stitch. "Just leave the goddamned thing alone!" The two would argue away, while Stitch stood in the shower, naked and vulnerable, trying to save his dignity by covering his private parts with his hands. "And don't take so goddamned long! Just get cleaned and then get the hell out." It was a typical conversation for the two whenever Stitch was in the shower.

It was a Friday evening and the "Good Shows" were going to be on. That's what Stitch and his sister, Caitlin and their little brother, Earl called the Friday Night line up, 'The Good Shows'. They would gather around the television to watch "Bewitched" and "The Partridge Family" and "The Brady Bunch" which were all on the same evening. The best part was when Aunt Teri and Uncle Danny would visit with Stitch's mom and dad from next door. All the adults would all sit out on the front stoop to drink beer, smoke cigarettes and talk and laugh, while the kids were upstairs, watching the television. If the kids were really good, they would get a small bowl of chips and a cup of Pepsi cola or possibly some ice cream. It was just a way to keep the kids out of the adults' hair, but regardless, Stitch always looked forward to Friday nights.

Stitch's sister, Caitlin, was sitting in the middle of floor with her legs at her side and pointing backwards. It was the weirdest thing Stitch had ever seen in all of his nine years of life. Most kids sat with their legs crossed in front of them. But not his sister Caitlin; she sat with her legs angled outward and her feet behind her. "Doesn't that hurt?" Their cousin Danielle asked Caitlin. Danielle was the same age as Stitch. As a matter of fact, they were born just five hours apart from one another. Stitch was born on June 20th, 1964 and Danielle on June 21st, 1964. The two of them grew up next door to one another and were more like brother and sister than cousins. Stitch sat on the sofa, watching Samantha Stevens twinkle her nose and create havoc for her husband, Darren, just as she did every week. However, this time it was harder for Stitch to watch because his sister's head was in his way.

"Will you two PLEASE move over so I can see the television?" Stitch asked as he tried to maneuver around his sister's head. It seemed that each time he would shift to the right, her head would end up falling to the right and if he moved back to the left, she would eventually bring her head over to the left. It's important to remember that this was 1973 and televisions weren't up on stands or hanging on the walls. In these days, the television sat on short legs and settled on the floor. Stitch's father made a modest living as a machinist and was able to purchase an RCA floor model, color television. It was a terrific television in its day. That is unless you had a sister who would sit like a freaking duck right in front of the screen. Caitlin snapped her head around and shot Stitch the most evil of eyes and said, "I WAS HERE FIRST! If *you* don't like it, you move!" and then she calmly turned to Danielle to answer her question. "Actually, sitting like this is very comfortable."

Stitch grew rage at his sister. There were times when he wondered if he could ever get along with her. She was always doing things to make him angry. She would humiliate him, torment him and if he tried to hit her, she would yell for their mother. Stitch always felt like he was caught between a rock and a hard place. "*If I beat her up, then Mom and Dad will punish me; and if I wait until we're adults and then beat her up, the cops will arrest me*!" he muttered to himself as he maneuvered to get a better view of the television. *I can't win!* He thought to himself.

Danielle moved from the floor up to the sofa to sit next to Stitch. "School is almost over." She said without taking her eyes from the television.

"I know. I can't wait." Stitch replied as he picked a potato chip from her bowl.

"You know what that means, dontcha'?" she said.

"Our birthdays are coming." Stitch replied with a smile.

"Oh my god," Danielle said with restrained excitement. "We're gonna be NINE-Years-Old!"

"That's almost TEN!"

"Two numbers!!" Danielle said with glee. "That's almost teenager!"

"What are you hoping to get for your birthday?" Stitch asked.

"I want an art set." said Danielle, "You know, with paints and markers and things like that. I'm gonna be an artist when I grow up." She took a sip of her soda and then asked him what he wanted.

"I want a Johnny West Action Figure, or an Evel Knievel Motorcycle guy!" Stitch said with excitement. He'd seen the commercial on TV, where all you had to do was pull the action ripcord and send Evel Knievel over jumps. "That would be so cool!"

"Will you guys SHUT UP?" Caitlin said without even turning around. Caitlin was a year younger than Stitch and Danielle, but acted like she was queen of the house. She was always making demands and starting arguments. But all of that goes with the territory of having a little sister and being the oldest. In Stitch's mind, Danielle had it easy because she was the baby of her family with an older brother. She was always being coddled and pampered, while Stitch was being told to set a good example for his younger siblings. As much as he envied Danielle's position, he wouldn't trade with her. Not for anything in the world. Except for an Evel Knievel Motorcycle guy, perhaps.

These were the memories caused by grasping an old, wooden banister, which were brought to Stitch's mind. He took a step up the stairs and smiled as it creaked under his weight.

As Stitch entered her kitchen, he had to stop for a moment as he realized that so much had changed. It was a bit overwhelming to be standing someplace that he hadn't been in so many years. The stove was exactly where he remembered it and he envisioned the nine-year-old version of himself lying on top of a trash bag, next to the stove, where his father had pushed him down. Stitch shrugged off the image and turned to see that she put her kitchen table in the same spot that Stitch's mother had kept their table when they lived there. Immediately he remembered many-a-card games at that table. His aunts and uncles would come over and play *Penny Ante Poker* with his mother and father, and he with his cousin Danielle would crawl under the table picking up the pennies that would drop to the floor and would save them for a trip to the corner candy store the next day. The walls were different; they didn't have the red and green-checkered tile along the chair boarder. The Cabinets were now wooden instead of the white metal boxes that he remembered. Stitch smiled as he recalled how he used to love waking up in the morning and coming down the stairs, through the front hall and into the kitchen where he would climb up on the counter to get a bowl of cereal. The cabinets were always cold to his touch. The plain stainless steel handles would show his fingerprints after he removed his hands. Now they were wood and glass and you could actually see what was in the cabinet without having to open it first. The floor was tiled, rather than the linoleum that used to bubble up in the summer. As he stood there looking around, the woman offered him a seat at the table. Stitch sat down and was happy to see the aluminum cast ceiling was still in place. It still had the Easter egg borders that he remembered.

The woman poured two cups of coffee and brought them to the table where she placed one cup in front of Stitch and placed the other in front of a seat, which she took. He watched the woman drink her coffee as he sat with his cup in front of him. He simply looked at it and tried to think of a polite way to decline but didn't have the heart to tell her that he couldn't stand the smell of the foul, putrid, dark liquid. Despite the fact that it was making his stomach do flip-flops, he didn't want to seem ungrateful or ignorant. So he just carried on the conversation as if he was comfortable with the drink. "How long have you lived here?" Stitch asked as he stirred the foul, devil fluid with a spoon.

She paused from bringing the cup to her lips. "Maybe four or five years." She said just before taking a sip of coffee. She looked up as she gave it more thought. "We moved here when Steven was five years old and he's going to be ten next month."

"He's your nephew?" ***Why did I ask that question?*** He thought to himself before speaking again. "I don't mean to be forward, I apologize."He gave a small, nervous laugh to hide his embarrassment.

"No, no." She said, waving it off as nothing. "Steven's mother was a single parent, she never knew his father..." She suddenly looked embarrassed as she had thought how absurd that statement sounded and then she explained how her sister led a wild life of drugs, alcohol, and many men. When she became pregnant, she had planned to terminate it, but could never go through with the abortion.

"She thought having the baby would help her to straighten out her life, but it only made things worse." The woman took a breath and exhaled, trying to forget whatever horrible memory she had just conjured forward. "Anyhow, Steven lives with me now and the two of us are happy just the way we are."

Stitch felt like a shit for prying and made sure to apologize to her. "I'm really sorry." I said. "I didn't mean to pry."

"It's all right, really." She said with a smile. "I must sound like a lunatic - inviting a stranger into my home, and spewing on about my personal life." She laughed an uncomfortable laugh. "I should be apologizing to you!"

"No apologies are necessary." He said. "I'm grateful for you allowing me into your home. Every childhood memory I have is wrapped up in the walls of this apartment." Stitch smiled as he thought about his childhood. "I loved living here." he calmly said without even realizing it; but he didn't even need to say so. She could see it in his eyes as he spoke.

"Would you like to see the rest of the apartment?" She asked.

Stitch smiled and eagerly stood up from his seat. "I thought you'd never ask." He replied with a small laugh.

She led him through the dining room where he paused and looked at the china hutch and the round wooden table. Above the back chair was a set of dark windows that looked out into the front hall. "This used to be my bedroom when I was very, very young." He spoke as if he was in a trance. Suddenly in his mind's eye, the table and chairs turned into a small trundle bed with a toy box situated at the foot of the bed. He turned around to another door and touched it as he remembered, "This is where my parents used to sleep."

"It's a hallway now." The woman replied opening up the door and showing a set of stairs going up. "There are stairs in there that go to the attic bedrooms."

"We used to have to go through the kitchen and out into the hallway and use those stairs." He told her as he walked towards the kitchen door to visualize what he remembered. "But I guess my Uncle Paulie must have seen that as a problem." It used to be set up that anyone off the street could have walked into the front hall, up the front stairs and then could have gone up the next set of stairs and into the bedrooms. As a little kid, this never dawned on Stitch, but now it seemed pretty unbelievable to think about it.

"Actually," she started. "I saw it as the problem". She explained her fear of the old set up, "anyone could walk in off the street and go up into the bedrooms."

Immediately another memory crept into Stitch's brain...

DECEMBER 1973

In 1973, when most of Stitch's family lived on Cataract street, no one ever worried about things like burglaries and break-ins. The big, green door never locked and no one ever thought about someone getting up into the bedrooms, and Stitch's cousin Vine counted on this when he heard that Stitch had stayed up late one night to watch a scary movie.

While Stitch and his brother and Sister were in the living room watching television, and Leon and Gerti were sitting in the Kitchen with Dan and Terri, Vince snuck up the attic stairs and actually hid under the Stitch's bed and waited patiently for him to go to sleep. After his usual routine of turning on and turning off lights, Stitch finally climbed into his bed, which was situated under the sloping ceiling of the attic all the while he had no idea his cousin Vince was lurking beneath it in wait. Stitch pulled the covers up to his shoulders and snuggled into his mattress, trying to make it warm. He could hear the cold December wind, blowing outside of the narrow bedroom window. Stitch turned to look out the window and noticed the power lines as they swayed in the wind and were weighted down with ice and snow. Stitch shuddered as he realized the icicles looked like the fangs of a giant creature. He closed his eyes and tried to get rid of the scary images but something fell onto Stitch's stomach. His eyes flew open, but before he could look and see what it was that landed on him the "thing" grabbed at his stomach. *IT'S A HAND*!! Stitch thought to himself in horror! Without even thinking, he jumped up, screaming but slammed his head on the angled ceiling and fell to the floor. He laid there for a moment, getting his senses back when he heard something shuffle under his bed and immediately Stitch jumped up and ran out through the bedroom door and down the stairs, three steps at a time! As he rounded the second floor, he used the banister as leverage to keep from falling down and he ran down the last set of stairs and out the front hall door!

Stitch jumped off the stoop and hurdled over a snow bank as he ran out into the street so he could look up at his bedroom window. From the safety of the street he tried to find out what was in his room. Suddenly, Stitch's mother threw up the living room window and yelled down at him. "What the fuck are you doing outside in your underwear?" Suddenly Stitch realized he was standing in the middle of the street in his tighty whities and nothing else. His little, skinny arms were crossed over his scrawny chest as he tried to keep himself warm from the cold December night wind. Thinking back on that memory, he thought, *I must have looked like an idiot, standing in snow and ice with nothing but my K-Mart underwear!* As the fear started to fade and embarrassment set in, Stitch heard a familiar laugh coming from the front hall. Soon, his cousinVince came out from the hall, laughing hysterically as he recalled his little cousin flying down the stairs leaving behind a fruit of the loom blur. At the time, Stitch was not amused. However, he found the memory quite amusing and smiled to himself as he recalled this event.

The kind woman looked at him as if trying to decipher the expression on his face. Stitch told her the story, to which she laughed and said, "Were you always so easily scared?" Stitch smiled as he noticed her sofa was in the same place where his parents kept their sofa. He invited her to sit as he told her just how much his family loved to scare one another...

CHAPTER TWO

October 10th 1973

It was late and Stitch was sitting up watching the *ABC Movie of the Week*, which was a horror picture, entitled "Don't Be Afraid of the Dark". It was a Thursday night and Stitch had school the next day; however, he had seen the previews for this show and really wanted to see it. It was a movie that was being aired for the Halloween season, which he had been waiting for weeks to see. His Mother didn't want him to watch the show, concerned that he'd have nightmares and wouldn't sleep. Stitch brushed it off, claiming that it was silly and he was NINE-years-old and only babies would be afraid of a movie. But his mother was smart and told him he could watch it if he wanted to, believing full and well that he would turn off the television after the first frightening scene and run off to bed. On that particular night she was going to Bingo with Aunt Terri and her sister, Percy. Stitch would be left at home with his father while his mother and his aunts went to BINGO. However, when the movie started, Stitch's father said he was going to get a bag of potato chips and would be right back. Stitch was excited about getting snacks for the movie, but sitting in the dark living room, with only the ominous glow of the television to keep him company was a little eerie. His brother and sister were upstairs, sleeping which meant he was alone watching one of most horrific movies he'd ever seen. The movie was about a young couple that inherited a family house. But the house was possessed by little, munchkin-like monsters that were hell bent on making the woman, (Sally), one of their own. As they crawled out from the fireplace, they would call to her in an eerie whisper of collective voices, "*Sally, Sally, Sally… We want you, want you, want you!*" Stitch pulled his feet from the floor and pulled his knees close to his chest as he watched in horror. Part of him wanted to close his eyes, but another part of him insisted he keep them open and watch or he'd miss something important. The woman fought back, against the little demons and when she realized that they were vulnerable to light, they found a way to cut the power. She tried to use flashlights and even tried using a camera's flash bulb. But the demons drugged her and tied her up and carried Sally off to the fireplace and dragged her down to a secret room of the house where they made her one of them.

By the end of the movie, Stitch's father still had not returned from getting potato chips. Afraid to get off the sofa, Stitch sat up and watched the news, trying to get the horrible images out of his mind. He wanted to forget about the fact that the very house they lived in was an old, family house. He wanted to forget about the dark basement under the stairs and the dark hallway that he had to navigate in order to get to his bedroom.

The news ended and Stitch noticed the clock read nearly midnight. His mother would be coming home from Bingo soon and his father was still out getting potato chips, or so he thought. In actuality, Leon went to the Orchard and went to a bar for a couple of beers. In Leon's mind, since the corner stores were closed, the bar was the only logical place where he could get a bag of chips. That's how Leon justified it to himself, anyhow. And since all his drinking buddies were there that was reason enough to stop and have a couple beers while playing pool and hustling some kids out of their drinking money. Stitch's father may have worn thick, horned rimmed glasses, but he could shoot a mean game of pool when he wanted to. There were times when he would go out drinking and come home with his paycheck doubled, just from hustling pool. There were other times when he'd come home with no paycheck, from being hustled at pool. Stitch's father was, by no means, a shark, but when he got a few beers in him, he couldn't turn down the opportunity to make a few bucks on the green felt tabletops.

Stitch heard the downstairs door slam shut and the sound of footfalls racing up the stairs. As the kitchen door opened and shut, his father quickly appeared in the dining room as if trying to win a foot race. "Is your mother home yet?" He asked as he came to a sliding stop and entered the pallor, half out of breath.

"Not yet." Stitch replied all the while looking for the small bag of potato chips that his father promised to bring back. "Where are the chips?" He asked.

"Forget the friggin' chips." His father slurred. "Just git yer ass to bed before your mother gets home. She'll wring my neck if you're still awake; you have school tomorrow."

Stitch jumped up and ran through the kitchen and out into the hallway. He stopped at the foot of the stairs and looked up into the vast darkness of the upstairs hallway. Taking a breath to settle his nerves, he quickly ran to the top of the stair and felt around for the light. It was a pull-chain style light that was hung from the ceiling, which caused him to fumble nervously in the dark to find it. He let his eyes adjust to the darkness and eventually found the small chain and pulled it, releasing the flood of light into the hallway at the top of the stairs. Stitch knew his father would get angry if he left the light on all night long. So he ran to his bedroom, where his younger brother was sleeping and turned on the bedroom light, which woke Earl up, rubbing his eyes. "HEY!"

Stitch didn't have the time to explain to his little brother, so he ran back down the hallway and turned the hall light off, but the bedroom didn't cast enough light to ensure Stitch's safety back down the hallway. He FROZE with fear in the middle of the hallway where there were closets on both sides of him and he could feel the tiny, glowing eyes of the Munchkin Monsters staring at his ankles. As the feeling started to engulf him, adrenaline kicked in and without even thinking about it he ran down the hallway and into his bedroom while slamming the door shut. Earl was sitting up with an angry look on his little face. "Why'd you turn the light on?" he asked.

"There are munchkins in the hallway that want to take us down to the basement!" Stitch said as he pulled the covers over his head. He didn't even stop to think if Earl would understand, he just blurted out what was scaring him and took refuge under his covers. Earl just sat there, in the middle of his bed wondering what the hell his older brother was talking about. Suddenly, the sound of footsteps in the hallway grew closer and closer to their door. Stitch sat up with a surprised look on his face. He turned to his brother who suddenly believed the footsteps belonged to Munchkin Monsters. The two of them jumped under their covers at the same time. Stitch realized his bedroom light was still on and the little munchkin demons wouldn't come in as long as the light was on, or so he thought. His bedroom door creaked open and Stitch froze with fear. As he held his breath, he waited to hear the little demons call his name in that frightening collective whisper. Instead, he heard his father's voice. "What the hell is going on up here?"

Stitch and Earl both threw their covers off their head and looked up at their father with surprise and relief. "Why is this goddamned light still on?" he bellowed.

"Stitch came in here and turned it on!" Earl said in a whine. "He woke me up."

"I couldn't see anything!" Stitch cried back.

"SHUT UP and go to sleep!" Leon yelled out in frustration. "Or the next time I come up here, I'll knock your fuckin' heads together!" Leon reached up and turned off their bedroom light when Earl started to cry. "What are you crying about?" Leon asked with annoyance. The last thing he needed was for Gerti to come home and see that the boys were still awake after midnight on a school night. Leon may have been taller and the man of the family, but Gerti was the one with the iron fist. Whenever Leon tried to show dominance, Gerti would knock him down a few pegs and on this particular night Leon didn't need any reason for Gerti be upset with him.

"Stitch said that monsters are going to drag us down to the basement."

"For Christ's sake, Stitch!" His father turned the light back on and crouched down as he approached Stitch's bed. It was situated along the front wall and under the slope of the roof. If Stitch sat up too quickly, he'd actually bang his head off his ceiling. He thought it was so cool to have a room with a sloping ceiling but at that moment he'd have given his left arm for a set of bunk beds to keep his father from swinging his hand against his ass. Stitch edged to the far side of his bed to get away from his father's swing. "Knock it off; I'm not gonna to hit you!" Leon said as he reached out to tuck Stitch into his bed. "Just quit scaring your brother, will ya." Stitch came up from under his covers and looked up at his dad.

"Will you leave the hall light on?" he asked sheepishly.

Leon looked over at his son but his face wasn't angry. He didn't' smile but he didn't yell. "All right, but it goes off when I go to bed, do you understand?"

Both Earl and Stitch nodded in unison and agreed to go straight to sleep so their father left the door ajar and retreated to the downstairs.

It was quiet upstairs. In the cold October evening, the wind was blowing outside the window by Stitch's bed and it made a small whistling noise. Stitch pulled the covers over his head and turned his back to the window.

"Stitch?" Earl whispered. "What's that noise?"

"It's just the wind." Stitch replied from under his covers. The two young boys tried to ignore the sound, but Earl couldn't get over it.

"Stitch." He whispered again.

"What?" Stitch had enough on his mind; he certainly didn't need anything added to it by his little brother.

"Will you sleep with me?"Earl asked.

Stitch thought about getting out of bed, but he knew if he put his feet down on the floor, the monsters would surely get him. "You come over here and sleep with me."

"No!" Earl exclaimed.

"Ssshhhh" Stitch was afraid their father would hear. "Hold on, I gotta get something." Stitch's hand fumbled around on the top of his desk in the dark. When he found what he was searching for, he darted from his bed and jumped onto Earl's bed without ever touching the floor. "Move over." Stitch said, trying to get the spot by the door. As Earl moved over towards the wall, Stitch leaned over the bed and situated his '*Johnny West*' action figure in a standing position while holding a rifle. Stitch had long dreamt for this toy and when he received it on his birthday, it was the happiest day of his young life and now Stitch would put Jonny West to stand guard at the doorway. He balanced the action figure with its rifle in both hands to scare away any munchkin monsters that might try to get into their room. "Don't worry, Earl." Stitch said to reassure his little brother. "I made sure nothing would come into our room now." Stitch believed that by placing the action figure at the door, it would frighten off any little munchkin demon and the boys were able to fall asleep.

It was 6:45 am and Stitch's mother came into the room to wake the boys for school. However, as she approached their bedroom door she noticed a small toy cowboy standing in the doorway. She smiled at the sight of it and bent down to pick it up; however, Stitch immediately woke up.

"NO!" he shouted.

His mother looked surprised. "What are you doing in your brother's bed?"

Stitch tried to think of a good reason. After all, it was his mother who told him that he shouldn't watch the movie and he wasn't about to prove her right. "Earl was scared and wanted me to sleep with him."

Gerti believed no such thing but indulged her son. "What's this for?" she said, holding up the toy cowboy.

"What's *that* for?" he repeated in a nervous tone as he tried to think of a proper answer.

"Yeah." She said, tossing the toy onto the bed next to him. "Why was this standing near the door?"

"Well..." he needed to think of something believable. He looked over to notice his brother was still asleep, so he whispered. "Earl was so scared; I told him that I would put it there so he could go to sleep."

"I see." She said, patronizing him. "But *you* didn't need it, right?"

Stitch let out a nervous laugh. "Me?" he said with mock surprise. "No, not me."

"Mm-hmm" She turned to leave the doorway saying, "Wake up your brother and be downstairs in 15 minutes for breakfast." As she turned to go wake up Caitlin, she laughed to herself at the sight of the cowboy, knowing the real reason her son put it in front of the door.

"I think I've seen that movie!" The pleasant woman said as she sat on the edge of her sofa listening to Stitch's story. However, she quickly changed the subject. "So I take it you went to through the school system around here?"

"I started at St. Patrick's and eventually to Abram Lansing's elementary and on up through the middle school and then Cohoes High School before leaving for the Navy."

"Steven goes to Abram Lansing's." She said as her nephew entered the room.

"You musta' gone there back in the black and white days." The young boy said innocently.

Stitch smiled as he recalled his childhood days and going to school at Abram Lansing's.

Stitch's school wasn't a far walk from his home. His mom would walk Stitch and his sister Caitlin to the schoolyard and pick them up afterwards. As they approached the playground of Abram Lansing's school, Stitch would normally dart off to join his friends. However, today his mother stopped him. His sister Caitlin was a grade behind him and her class was to finish at noon; while, Stitch had a full day of class. "Uncle Greg is going to pick you up from school today." His mother told him as she straightened the collar of his jacket. "You're to wait right here until he shows up, do you understand?" Greg was Gerti's little brother who was just six years older than Stitch. Greg was in High School and promised he would walk down to the elementary school to pick up his nephew on his way home from school.

"Yes." Stitch replied, while looking at the playground over his mother's shoulder. He was eager to get to his friends so he could play before the bell rang.

"I'm not kidding young man!" She said sternly while waving her index finger at him. "You wait right here until Uncle Greg shows up."

"Ok." He said with utter frustration and still looking over her shoulder at the playground in search of his classmates. "Can I go now?"

She let him go and walked his sister up to the school door. Stitch joined his circle of friends, which was literally a circle that the boys would stand in as they talk about things they did or games they played the night before. The play ground had three or four of these circles of all boys and a few circles of all girls. Those who weren't in circles were running around playing tag, or throwing sticks at Mitch Rogolphski or Marge Collington. Mitch was probably the dirtiest, smelliest of the boys and Marge was a fat, little, dirty haired, poorly dressed girl. They were outcasts and the jokes of the school that the cruel kids would use against one another. Boys would run up to girls and touch them while exclaiming, "MITCH GERMS!" and the girls would pretend to spray themselves with an antiseptic spray while chasing after the boys and touching them exclaiming, "LARGE MARGE GERMS!" However, Stitch would rather stand in his circle of friends which consisted of his best friend, Jared, whom he'd known since the second grade; Derrick Dodson, who sat behind Stitch and drew cartoons with him from time to time. There was also Thad Campbell, Dave Galicki and Todd Logan who were the other boys in Stitch's circle; and Stitch knew what he was going to talk about with his friends on that day. He was going to tell them about the movie he watched and how scary it was. Unfortunately for him, none of his friends had seen the movie so he couldn't get feed back from them and his story went over like a lead balloon. The other kids didn't understand the plot of the story because Stitch didn't really understand the movie. All he knew was the fact that there were scary munchkins in the movie.

"Munchkins?" Jared said, laughing at Stitch. "You mean like those funny little people on the Wizard of Oz?" Jared reached out and flicked Stitch on the tip of his nose with his middle finger as way of insulting him.

"No!" Stitch said defensively and pushing Jared's finger away from his nose. "They were smaller and scarier!"

"Oh my god!" Thad Campbell said loudly. "Yer a-scared of those gay, little munchkins!" The entire circle of boys started laughing at Stitch. It looked like it was going to be one of those days.

When school ended, Stitch waited outside for his sister's class to come out. It wasn't until all the kids were gone and he was standing alone that he realized that she had a half-day. "What did mom say to me?" He tried to recall her conversation with him, but couldn't remember it all. He cursed himself for not paying attention. He began thinking that he misunderstood his mother and that maybe he was supposed to meet his uncle someplace. He began walking down the hill from Abram Lansing's school. *I know my way home*, He thought to himself. *Mom and Uncle Greg will be really happy to see that I was able to walk home alone and they'll be ready to lift me up on their shoulders and cheer...YEAH! HE DID IT!! HE DID IT BY HIMSELF!*

Despite being delusional, he smiled proudly as he walked down the hill to the main street. But once he got there he realized that he didn't know where to go. The crossing guard was gone and he knew he needed to get across the busy street. He remembered his teacher telling the class they should wait until the light was green before crossing the street, so he waited patiently. Once the cars stopped, he stepped out into the road and felt as though he was stepping into uncharted territory. It was different for him and he felt bold and daring. He started to run when he wondered how long the light would remain green. He imagined that the cars would just start up and run him flat, like the animals on cartoons and he'd be a paper-thin boy, blown away with the breeze. As he jumped up on to the curb at the other side of the street, he felt a sense of accomplishment and he smiled proudly as he looked back at his starting point. Stitch turned north and began walking and looking for something that was familiar. He crossed a small side street and noticed a dry cleaner on the corner. Across from the dry cleaners was a coin operated laundry and next to that was the middle school, where the big kids went to school. *Where Uncle Greg went to school!* He thought if he waited there, his uncle would see him. So he waited some more. Still no Uncle Greg.

Stitch sat on the steps of the dry cleaners and bawled like a baby until a woman came out from the cleaners and brought him into the shop. She offered him a cookie and a cup of milk, and asked where he lived. *I know the answer to that question!* He should know it since his teacher would often test them on things like that.

"Number four Cataract Street" He told her through sobbing tears while spitting cookie crumbs through his words. He sniffled and felt a drain of snot back track from his upper lip and into his nose again. The kindly woman picked up the phone and dialed as he looked around the room. He noticed signs and price tags on displays and racks of clothes and ties.

The next thing Stitch knew, he was in a police car and they were driving him up to his house. "That's where I live!" He shouted to the police officer while pointing over his shoulder. "That's my home!"

When they let him out of the car, he looked up and noticed his mother in the window on the second floor. As she ran from the window, the curtains floated behind her and slowly fell back against the panes of glass. Suddenly Stitch became scared. He felt as though she would be angry for having the police bring him home in the cop car. The entire neighborhood of kids came around as Stitch climbed out of the police car and walked up to his stoop with a police officer. *They probably think I did something bad.* He thought to himself as his cousins and friends walked over to him. *They probably think I'm a crook or a bad-guy, or something like that.* Suddenly, Aunt Terri came outside to see what the commotion was about. It was around that time that his mother appeared through the front hall door and behind her was his Uncle Greg.

"WHERE THE HELL HAVE YOU BEEN, YOUNG MAN?" She exclaimed. "We've been worried sick!"

"I'm sorry." Stitch said, as tears welled up in his eyes.

"I was looking for you." Uncle Greg said from behind Stitch's mom. "I thought you were lost."

"He was lost." The police officer said. "A woman called us and asked us to bring him home." The police officer rubbed his hand against Stitch's hair. But he's a smart boy and he knew his address; just didn't know his phone number, otherwise we would have called you to let you know sooner that he was all right."

Stitch's mom bent down and scooped him up in a hug. This surprised Stitch, since he was expecting a scolding for trying to walk home on his own. "Don't you *EVER* do that again, young man! Do you understand me?"

Stitch was sobbing now, and all his friends were watching. "Yes!" He cried out. "I'm sorry." He didn't care who had seen him crying. He was just happy to be home.

Stitch's mom and Uncle Greg explained to the officer what was supposed to happen and the police officer tipped his hat politely and then got into his car and drove away. From that day on, Stitch would remember that police officers weren't just there to pick up the bad guys and put people in jail. They were there to help people as well. Never again would he be afraid of the police. From that day forward, he would have the utmost respect for the Officers of the Law.

"Would you care to see the upstairs?" The woman asked, leading the way into the room that used to belong to his parents. "The hallway stairs have been converted into storage space now." She said as she flipped on a light switch and led Stitch up to the bedrooms. He froze at the top of the stairs when he spotted a gas stove. It was the same old stove that heated the upstairs when he was a little kid.

"Does this still work?" Stitch asked.

"I don't think so." She replied. "The apartment has central air and heating now. It hasn't been used the entire time I've lived here."

Stitch remembered many a winter night, lying on the floor in front of the stove and watching the flames dance behind the Pyrex window at the bottom of the large, hulking mass. Sometimes, he would stand over it and spit down into it so he could hear his saliva sizzle on the pipes inside. "My mother always placed a pot of water on the top of this stove." He said smiling to the memory while he placed the palm of his hand on the top of the stove. "Looking back, I now realize it was to keep the air humid, but as a child, I always thought she did it just so she'd have hot water to use if she ever needed it." Mom never drank coffee, but she enjoyed tea sometimes. However, her favorite drink was Pepsi Cola. She would always have a bottle of Pepsi in the refrigerator and a huge jug of Kool-Aide for the kids. Suddenly, Stitch remembered something and started to laugh.

"What is it?" The woman asked as she heard Stitch laugh out loud.

He pointed to the room on the left. That was my mother's '*sitting room*' he told her. "She would go in there, with my Uncle Tim or Aunt Percy and they would watch television or play cards." Stitch began to reminisce about his mother's room, which was more like her fortress of solitude rather than just a sitting room to watch television.

"I'm not sure what year is was, but I remember my father was downstairs, changing my baby Sister Melanie's diaper. I was in my room, across the hall from my mother's sitting room when she called to me to go downstairs and get her a glass of Pepsi.

"Hey, Dipshit!" she called out. "Go downstairs and get me a glass of Pepsi." Gerti wasn't very diplomatic, but she was my mother so I just did as she told me. However, as I was heading down the stairs, my Uncle Tim yelled for me to get him a glass too, but he had done something to me earlier that made me angry…I can't remember what it was." Stitch stopped to think and then gave up, waving the issue away. "Anyways, I wanted to tell him no, because I was so mad at him, but I couldn't say no; so I went to go get them their Pepsi drinks. Just as I got to the stairs, Uncle Tim called out, "And don't forget to put ice it." When I got downstairs, I went to the refrigerator and I poured them the Pepsi. Since my father's back was turned to me I knew I had to take this opportunity to do '*something*' to get back at my Uncle Tim. So I picked up the saltshaker and put a ton of salt into my Uncle Tim's glass. If I learned anything about Pepsi from my mother is was that Salt and Pepsi does not go together. I walked up the stairs while remembering which glass was my uncle's and which was my mother's. I let myself into her room and handed mom her glass and then Uncle Tim his. He turned to me and said, 'What, no ice?' I just smiled and said. 'Sorry' and then turned and left. As soon as the door closed, I bolted down the stairs and then down to the back yard. I jumped the fence and ran to the park laughing. I only wish I could have seen their faces."

The woman laughed at the story. "What does Pepsi taste like when it's salted?" She asked in amazement.

"Trust me!" Stitch laughed. "You don't wanna know!" Stitch knew what it tasted like, and prayed he'd never taste that horror on his tongue ever again.

Stitch's Mother, Gerti, always said that the Pepsi was for the adults and the Kool-Aid was for the kids. However, Stitch's sister would always sneak into the kitchen with the stealth and cunning of a jewel thief; she would pop open the fridge and take a swig out of the Pepsi bottle not because she was thirsty, but because her mother told her it was forbidden. However, Gerti could never catch who was stealing her Pepsi, so she planted a decoy bottle of Pepsi in the fridge and, based on Stitch's prank on his Uncle Tim, she salted the Pepsi down. She knew she'd hear one of the kids complain about the awful tasting soda and then she'd have the culprit. One afternoon Caitlyn went into the kitchen and opened the Pepsi and took a swig and suddenly her face cringed up and she ran to the kitchen sink and spit the soda down the drain. Stitch laughed at her, thinking she got a snoot-full of bubbles or something.

"Serves you right." Stitch said with a chuckle.

"You taste that crap!" She said as she wiped her mouth dry. And, like an idiot, Stitch did just as she suggested. He slowly and quietly cracked open the door to the refrigerator and then quietly twisted the cap from the Pepsi bottle and tip it up to his lips and took in a small sip when he was suddenly horrified by a taste that can barely be described accurately. Stitch threw the bottle back into the refrigerator door and ran to the sink and spit out the foul tasting soda as he cried out, "Aww, man! That stuff is awful!" Just then a rapid pounding of the floor boards could be heard, as well as felt, as Gerti ran from the living room and into the kitchen where she found Stitch bent over the sink spitting out the salted fluid.

"You little bastard!" She yelled as she entered the kitchen and found Stitch still leaning over the sink. "So you're the one whose been drinking my Pepsi!"

Stitch turned around to point out his sister, but she was smart enough to be gone at that point. Just another reason he envied his cousin Danielle.

After a brief tour of the upstairs, Stitch stopped near the door that, as a child, Stitch used to come up from the kitchen entrance. It was bolted shut but as he stood there looking at it, he realized he was standing between the two closets that used to scare the crap out of him. A shiver went up and down his spine as if touched by the cold finger of death. Quickly, Stitch moved backwards, towards the stove all the while keeping his focus fixed into the dark area. Above, on the ceiling, was the hanging light that he used to have to reach for in the dark. Stitch suddenly remembered why he put salt in his uncle's drink...

Stitch was on his way to bed and it was the same routine as it had been every night since he had watched that horrible, Halloween movie. He would turn on the light at the bottom of the stairs and then run to the top to turn on the light between the two closets and then run back down the stair to turn off the hall light and then back up stairs to make his way to his bedroom. It was worse since Vince had decided to scare him. Gerti nearly beat the shit out of Vince for what he did, but Vince was proud! However, on this particular night, when Stitch reached the light, he pulled the string but nothing happened. He pulled it, again and again, but still no light. He called down to his father to let him know the bulb was burned out, but his father only told him to go to bed. He knew he couldn't leave the downstairs hall light on, but he had to have some light to get to his room, otherwise the tiny munchkin demon monsters would get him! He became nervous as he descended the stairs. He would have to turn off the light and then walk up the stairs in the dark. Even worse, he would have to pass by the two closets with no light to check for munchkin demons. He took a breath, switched off the hall light at the foot of the stairs, and slowly crept up on his hands and knees. He had two reasons for doing the low crawl; first he thought if anything was going to come at him, he needed to be low and out of its way and second if he crawled he would make less noise going up the stairs. But then he realized that the munchkin demons were tiny and that by being on his knees, he was giving them a chance to jump on his face. Stitch quickly jumped up and ran to the top of the stairs. When he got there, he stood by the doorway that led into the hall between the two closets. He could feel the demons watching him from the closets and he could almost hear them breathing and snickering at him. Was sure he was imagining it, but he was also sure that he could *really* hear them. Stitch inched his way closer to the closets. As he approached the doorway he was positive there was something in there. Something that was dangerous. He could feel them looking at him and his body was suddenly filled with adrenaline. He immediately bolted across the floor, barely even touching the cold linoleum with his feet. When he got to his room he made a leaping bound to his bed in just two steps and dove under his covers. His heart was racing and his breathing was out of control. He tried to hold his breath. *If they think I'm dead, they won't want me*. He thought to himself. Stitch held his breath as long as he could, but eventually exhaled and took a few more breaths before holding it. However, he was noisy about it and surely the munchkin demons would hear his heavy breathing. He needed to listen for them and he couldn't hear over his own breathing or heart beat. He tried to calm himself so he counted in his head. Suddenly he heard something! It was a whisper! *OH MY GOD THEY'RE HERE!* He thought to himself. He held his breath to hear better and sure enough he heard that awful, nasty whisper as it called his name.

"Stitch – Stitch – Stitch!" He trembled under his covers and prayed to god to make them go away.

"We want you – want you – want you!" Suddenly they weren't just calling his name; they were scratching at the door.

THEY'RE COMING TO GET ME! He wanted to scream, but he couldn't. He was so full of fear that he felt as though he would wet himself.

"Stitch – Stitch – Stitch!" They called again. From deep inside, Stitch mustered up as much courage as he could and he sat up in bed and screamed, "MOM!!!!" But he heard a creaking noise. It was his door opening. Terror filled his little body! He needed to get help. He took one last breath and then... "MOMMY!!" He screamed out at the top of his lungs and jumped up, hitting his head off the sloping ceiling. Now he was crying and whimpering like a little girl. He listened again, but there was nothing except for laughter and then footfalls running down the stairs. It was his Uncle Tim! He had been hiding in the closet, waiting for Stitch to get to bed just for the purpose of being able to scare him with his most horrible of fears. Stitch sat in the middle of his bed crying. He was not just upset by the fact that he was scared and embarrassed, but he was saddened by the fact this own Uncle would go out of his way to frighten a nine-year-old, and take pleasure in that fact. Stitch felt ashamed and angry both at the same time. He wanted to lash out and retaliate but his Uncle was huge and Stitch had always been afraid of that man. But he knew one day he would pay him back for scaring him. One day he would make his uncle sorry he ever scared him so badly. He didn't know when or how he would do it but he was certain that such a day would come.

"Are you ok?" The woman said as she touched his arm. Stitch literally jumped and spun around looking as white as a ghost. "Oh my god!" she gasped. "What's wrong?"

"Just a bad memory." Stitch replied as the color slowly returned to his face. He took a refreshing breath before speaking, "But I'm ok now, thanks." He smiled nervously and walked back to the stairs, afraid that he might have scared the woman and she may want him to leave her house at this point.

In the living room, the woman brought Stitch a glass of water with ice, rather than a request to leave as he thought she might. "Your coffee went cold, so I thought you might like some iced water." She said as she handed him the glass.

"Thank you." Stitch sipped at the glass and looked over at Steven, her nephew, who was sitting on the floor playing a video game. Stitch smiled as he recalled the days of his own youth. There were no video games during his childhood; nor were there computers or Internet. All he had was the television with perhaps four channels to watch. "It's amazing what kids have available to them these days." Stitch said as he watched the game play out on the television screen.

"He loves those video games." The woman replied. "I tell him he needs to get out and play more, but he'd rather sit at home and play those silly games." Steven continued to play as if he were oblivious to their conversation while the game on the television screen showed a woman, holding a gun and shooting zombies. The game was graphic, with blood spewing out of the zombies and the blasting sound of the gun as Steven pushed the correct buttons on his controller. Stitch shook his head in disbelief of the animated horror. "How many kids live on this street now?" Stitch asked without looking away from the television.

"I'm not sure, to be quite honest." The woman replied. "He has a couple of friends, but they don't come over all that often."

"That's because they're all butt-heads" Steven said. "I don't need them anyway."

"You don't like the other kids on the block?" Stitch asked with some surprise. After all, when he was a kid on this block, most of the kids that lived here were family. There were some jerks, but for the most part, everyone got along.

"Would you like kids that made fun of you all the time?" Steven answered absently. However, he had no idea that Stitch knew all too well what it was like to be a kid who wasn't popular. Stitch recalled how drastically his life had changed once his father lost his vision and had to leave work. There were no more weekly paychecks coming into the house, only monthly Social Security Disability checks that would come in. Life, as the LeRue family knew it, had changed forever when Leon lost his job.

CHAPTER THREE

July 23rd 1976

The sun was hot on this particular Friday and everyone was sitting outside, and trying to keep cool. Stitch was playing baseball in the local park with his brother, Earl and the rest of the neighborhood kids. Stitch's cousin, Danielle wanted to play, but he argued that girls were not good baseball players and that she should be in the stands, cheering for the boys. That didn't sit well with Danielle and she demanded to play ball but all the other boys voted against her.

Stitch was at bat and waiting for just the right pitch when Freddy released an overhand lob just as Stitch liked it; low and outside. Stitch gripped his bat, but not too tightly as he put his weight on his back leg and then leaned into the pitch and he slammed it hard and high. He was please as he heard the ball crack against the bat. As he finished his swing, he heard another crack and he froze along with everyone else on the field. He turned to see Danielle standing behind him with her hand over her mouth and blood pouring down between her fingers. Everything was silent for a moment and Stitch could only hear his pulse pounding in his ears. Suddenly, a siren like wail began to shriek from Danielle as she looked at her hands and noticed all the blood. She immediately turned and ran from the park and across Mohawk street and into her house. Stitch became scared and thought he'd get punished for hitting her with the baseball bat.

"But it was an accident!" he yelled as everyone looked from him to the small puddle of blood and dirt on the field. "I didn't know she was standing behind me, really!" Stitch became scared because he knew his mother would kick his ass for hitting his cousin with a baseball bat. He felt as though he needed to get home and fix the problem before it got out of hand. He dropped the bat and ran to his house as fast as he could. He was afraid of what might happen, but he imagined if he told his mother what happened before the news came from Aunt Terri or Uncle Dan, it wouldn't be so bad.

As Stitch ran to his house, Danielle ran into the front hall door of her house. She flew up the stairs and into her kitchen all the while, screaming as if she'd just witnessed a murder. Her mother and father came running into the kitchen, from the living room, to see what had happened and were shocked to see Danielle dancing around in the middle of the kitchen, holding her bloody hands over her mouth and screaming and crying. Her father, who was now a nervous wreck, tried to calm her down.

"What happened?" he asked her with restrained panic as he placed his hands on the sides of her head, trying to get her steady. But she kept running in place and screaming. Her words were unintelligible. "Danielle!" he said louder, "Danielle, what wrong? What happened?" Danielle's mother was getting nervous. She did the only thing she knew to do when she was nervous or scared; she yelled.

"Danielle Marie Lafayette, you answer your father right now!" Whenever Aunt Terri used the middle name, you just had to know she was not kidding.

Danielle seemed to calm down enough to get some words out. "Ah wathbit wiff a bot!" she said through her busted mouth and bloody lips.

"You were bit by a bat?" her father repeated back. "How the hell did a bat bite your mouth?" He began wondering if he heard her correctly, while at the same time trying to remember where his car keys were so he could take his daughter to the hospital. But Danielle shook her head and tried again.

"Ah wazz it wiff a bot" she said slower, trying to hold back the pain so her father could hear her better.

"Where did the bat bite you, honey?" Her mother asked. She looked at Dan who returned her worried look.

"Sthitth it may wiff a baht" Danielle said again. This time she was a little clearer for Dan to hear.

"Stitch hit you with a bat?" Dan repeated back. Danielle nodded her head and then clasped her hands back over mouth.

"That's just silly!" Terri said. "Gerti wouldn't let little Stitch have a pet bat!" She gave Danielle a scolding look. "You better tell us what really happened, young lady, or there's gonna be trouble!"

"A BATHE BAW BAHT!" Danielle said slower and rolling her eyes at her mother's misunderstanding.

"WHAT!" Terri screamed. "Why did he hit you with a baseball bat?"

"It was an accident, Mom." Vince said, as he walked into the house. "They were playing baseball and Danielle walked up behind little Stitch as he was swinging the bat." Even though Vince was a few years older than Stitch and Danielle, Stitch always felt a special bond with Vince. This was just one of those reasons why. Now there were times when Vince did some things to Stitch that most kids would never forgive. Like scaring him into running out into the street in his underwear! But Vince was like the older brother that Stitch never had, and to forgive him was easy for Stitch. There was one instance when Stitch and Vince were wrestling around on Aunt Terri's bed and Vince accidentally threw Stitch into the book-case headboard, causing Stitch to get four sutures in his head. There was also a time that Vince and Stosh threw Stitch, head long down a hill on a sled and crashed him face first into the brick wall at the bottom, causing Stitch to lose his front tooth. He suffered a black eye and a nice welt on his forehead for a few days but afterwards, Stitch would always come back for more. He didn't care how banged up he got; he just wanted to hang with the older guys and be accepted by his cousin Vince.

Through the kitchen door, behind Vince, came Stitch and his mother. Stitch stood partly behind his mom and peeked out from behind her leg to see if Danielle was all right. Gerti pulled him out from behind her and pushed him towards his cousin. "What do you say?" She said. Although, it was more of a statement, than it was a question.

Stitch took a step towards Danielle and stared down at the floor. He nervously traced the pattern of the linoleum with the toe of his sneaker as he spoke. "I'm real sorry fer crushin you in the face with a baseball bat, Danielle." He said in a near whisper. "If you want…" he turned to look back at his mother for confirmation and she nodded to him to continue. "If you wanna hit me back, you can."

"Danielle!" Terri said with shock as her daughter contemplated the offer. "Don't you dare!"

"It was an accident, Aunt Gerti." Vince said as he turned towards his aunt. "I saw the whole thing."

"I *really* am sorry." Stitch spoke up. He turned and looked at his Uncle Dan and Aunt Terri. They both smiled, as they couldn't resist his little baby blues.

"Well, Vince gave you a bloody mouth in the past, right!" Dan said as he shook his hand over Stitch's hair. "As long as it wasn't fighting and there was no malice, everything will be ok." Physically, Uncle Dan reminded Stitch of Archie Bunker from '*All In the Family*'. But he didn't have the same rough, irritating personality as the TV character. He was a kind, warm and loving person. Stitch always enjoyed spending time with his Uncle Dan.

As Terri went to the freezer to get Danielle a rag of ice for her mouth, Danielle and Stitch waved good-bye for the day. He would have to go home and take a bath, and she would have to stay home and be cared for. But when you lived right next door to your cousins and friends, there would always be tomorrow.

When Stitch and Gerti returned to their home, Stitch's father was sitting at the kitchen table. His glasses were on the table next to a cup of coffee and he was rubbing his eyes with his thumb and forefinger.

"What are you doing home already?" Stitch's mother asked as she approached him with her hands on her hips. She was not a tall woman by any means, but she was larger than life. She exuded a presence that couldn't be ignored. When she laughed, you laughed with her and when she was angry, you stayed the hell away. Her Bright Red hair indicated her Irish temper which was not to be taken lightly. She was shorter than Stitch's father but she was stout. Stitch's father, Leon was tall and lean but he was a strong man. Stitch would sometimes stare at the veins that protruded through the skin on his father's hands and admire how masculine they looked. He would then look at his own hands, only to see tiny blue lines under his skin. To Stitch, his father was stronger than any other dad. But looking at him now, with his head down and his face in his hand, he didn't look strong. He looked defeated. As Gerti moved closer to him, Leon looked up and his eyes were red. Stitch was shocked, but he couldn't be sure if his dad was crying or just frustrated. He couldn't see any tears in Leon's eyes. Leon held out his right hand and showed it bandaged.

"What the hell happened?" Gerti asked. Stitch was surprised as her question had no compassion behind it. It was more accusatory than anything else.

"I got it caught in a machine, at work." He replied.

"YOU WHAT?" Gerti couldn't believe her ears.

"It's nothing serious." He said, trying to deflate the issue. "But when they sent me to the doctor, I had to get x-rays and then the doctor asked to check my eyes."

Leon had always had poor vision. He was in the Army when he was younger but had to be medically discharged for poor eye sight. It was a miracle that he got a job as a machinist with eyes like his. Despite his poor vision, he did a damned good job building doorframes and doors. He cut metal to precision and worked for many years for his company. Now they were threatening to let him go because of his vision.

"Why did they look at your eyes?" Gerti asked.

"Because they want to protect the company from any liability." Leon replied with a touch of anger. "In case I want to sue them."

"What did the doctor say"? She asked.

"I didn't understand everything, but I have to see an eye specialist." Leon reported.

"A specialist?" she asked more to confirm if what she heard was correct or not.

"Yeah." He said as he picked up his spoon and dipped it into the sugar. "They said I have pin holes or something, in my eye and it's causing me problems with my vision." He stirred the sugar into his coffee. Stitch winced at the smell of it.

"Well can you go back to work?" She asked with worry.

"I'm going in tomorrow and I'll probably be on desk work until I see the specialist. Once he clears me, I can return to my regular job."

"Is that what you *think* or that what they told you?" She wanted to make sure that he wasn't guessing and that he received this information from his Union rep.

Stitch stood there, listening to the banter between his parents. He didn't understand how someone could get holes in their eyes, but at the same time, he didn't like to think about his dad having holes in his eyes. Stitch just stood there and said nothing. He watched as his mother stood there and his father sat at the table. Gerti stood looking at her husband with her hands at her side. Leon sat at the end of the table with his face looking down at the tabletop. Stitch thought someone should hug but no one did. They just stood there for what seemed like an eternity. It wasn't until Earl ran into the kitchen, from the front hall that the tension broke.

"Did ya hear what Stitch did to Danielle?" he asked as he skipped in and threw his baseball glove into the living room. "Man! He got a home run off that slug!"

"Earl!" His mother said sternly. "Either go out and play or go to your room!" Gerti was clearly taken back by the news of her husband. What would happen if his lost his job? How would he get around if he were blind? Her mind was buzzing with thousands of thoughts, concerns, and scenarios. She certainly didn't need her nine-year-old son running through the kitchen tattle tailing on his brother.

"I wanna watch TV." He said with a slight whine.

"It's too hot to watch television." She countered. "Go out and play." She said through clenched teeth, trying to get the point across that this was not the right time. Stitch shot his little brother a quick look of warning, but Earl must have missed it.

"But it's too hot outside." Earl whined. His head limped forward, as if his neck had just given out and his arms wobbled at his side. At first, Stitch thought his brother was going to collapse, but then realized he was just exaggerating his frustration. As Earl spoke he walked over to the refrigerator, opened the door and leaned in, looking at the contents in the door. "Can I have some Pepsi?" he asked. His tone was renewed; there was no longer a whine in his voice. However, everyone including Leon, turned to look at Earl as if he was crazy. In the LeRue house, it was common knowledge that the Pepsi was Mom's and the Kool-Aid was for the kids. Earl looked up from the open door and realized this information as he seen his family looking at him with faces covered with shock and horror. With a look of disappointment, Earl said, "N'er mind I'll just have Kool-Aid."

August 13th 1976

For the past few weeks, Leon had seen eye doctor, after eye doctor and all confirmed the same thing. He was suffering from a condition known as detached retina. His driver's license was immediately taken away as he was no longer allowed behind the wheel of a car. Worse still, he lost his job and could not work any longer. He was forty-years-old and he was forced to retire. However, this retirement had no pension. He was forced to apply for Social Security Disability and Food Stamps. Leon retreated to the orchard and sat in Rocky's Bar & Grill drinking a beer.

"That's pretty screwed up, what they're doin' to you, Leon." Rocky said, as he poured Leon's beer from behind the bar. "How is it that your eyes became unattached?"

Leon smiled. "It's not that my eyes are unattached." He said before taking a swallow of the Amber fluid. "It's the retina or some friggin' thing that's *in* my eyes."

Leon was born in 1936. Not only was he born fifteen weeks premature, but he was also a twin. Twins are usually smaller in size, but premature twins were even smaller still. Stitch's grandfather often told tale of how Leon could be held in the palm of his hand when he was born. However, in 1936 incubators were a little more than metal bins with an oxygen tube. That is what caused the retinal detachment in Leon's eyes. High concentrations of oxygen exposure, while he was in the incubator, caused a breakdown in the retina of his eyes. Over the years, the retina began to deteriorate, which is the main reason for all his vision problems throughout his life. Forty years later, it had taken its ultimate toll and Leon was told he was slowly going blind. He had lost his job, and even if he didn't, he certainly couldn't drive to work. He felt useless; so he sat in Rocky's Bar & Grill trying to drink the useless feelings away.

Back in the LeRue house, Gerti had just put up some curtains that she purchased. However, the curtains didn't quite match the walls so she decided to paint the walls a new color so everything would match. In the back hall were all the paint cans and the tarp and other paint supplies. She picked the right color and looked for a brush; however, the only brush available to her was a tiny, one-inch brush. All of the larger brushes were crusted with dried paint. With a sigh, she decided to have at it with the one-inch brush. "It might take a little longer, but at least it'll get done." She told herself as she gathered up her materials.

It had been six hours when Gerti had finished the entire living room. She stood in the middle of the room and looked around with a proud smile on her face. The room looked wonderful in its new blue color and the curtains were the perfect compliment. She picked up the tarp and paint cans and her brush when she heard the downstairs door slam shut. She looked up at the clock and noticed it was well past 1 AM. Gerti dropped her painting supplied in the kitchen and stood ready to greet her husband. The hall light was out and she heard him fumbling up the steps and muttering to himself. She wanted to see if he would be able to notice the new color to the living room as well as the new curtains. She could tell he had been drinking and rather than cuss him out for his drinking, she decided to let him hang himself. She quickly gathered up the paint supplies and hid them in the pantry and then went into the living room to wait for him. The kitchen door opened and Leon staggered in, bumping his self between the kitchen counter and the stove. He walked over to the coffee pot and tapped at it with his fingers and felt it was still warm enough for drinking and poured the jet-black liquid into a large mug. He added his creamer and sugar before he took a sip. The taste was horrendous and Leon realized that this must have been sitting from early in the day. He looked through the dining room and into the living room and noticed the light from the television. "Gerti must still be awake," he said to himself. He straightened up and then lit a cigarette, hoping the smell combined with the coffee would hide the beer on his breath. He did his best to walk as straight as possible through the dining room and when he made it to the living room he looked at his wife who was sitting in a recliner, watching an old, black and white movie and he smiled at her. However, the room smelled funny to Leon, but he couldn't place the scent as it was mixed with coffee and cigarette. It was difficult for him to determine the smell of the fresh paint, over his stale coffee and cigarette, not to mention the booze. He walked across the pallor and around the coffee table and plopped down on the couch, nearly spilling his coffee in his lap. Gerti wanted to bolt up, but she remained steadfast in her seat, waiting for him.

"What the frig is that smell?" he said with a touch of slur to his speech. "Smells like a friggin' slaughter house." He commented.

Gerti bit her lip as she kept her eyes on the television. All night long, she dealt with four kids who wanted to eat, play and run through the house as she was trying to paint the living room with a one inch brush and make a nice home for them. Now her drunken husband didn't even notice the new curtains, let alone the freshly painted walls. "It's paint." She said without looking in his direction.

"PAINT!" he exclaimed. "Why the hell did you paint?"

At this point, Gerti jumped up out of her recliner and into the middle of the room and started questioning his whereabouts.

"Where they hell have you been, huh?" She pointed to the ceiling, indicating the children. "Do you know what I've been putting up with, while you've been out drinking" She started counting off with her fingers. "I've been Feeding the kids, cleaning the house, doing the laundry, putting up new curtains, AND PAINTING THIS ENTIRE ROOM WITH A FRIGGIN' TOOTHBRUSH!!"

"Toothbrush?" Leon's alcohol haze didn't understand her frustration. "Why the hell did you use a toothbrush, we have a paint brush in the back hall, you know." He stood up to show her what he believed she missed.

"I USED the paint brush, you simple bastard!" She said as she stormed into the kitchen and brought back the tiny, one-inch brush. "But this is all there was, because YOU never cleaned out the other brushes!" The argument turned heated and the two yelled at each other back and forth; louder and louder. Their voices carried to the upstairs and Caitlin was the first one to hear it and she sat up in her bed. She couldn't make out the words, but she definitely knew it was her mother and father as she'd heard these voices before. Suddenly, there was a blood-curdling scream. Heavy, pounding footsteps carried their way to the upstairs and Caitlin became scared. She ran into Stitch's room and woke up her older brother.

"Mom and Dad are fighting again!" She said as she shook him awake. Stitch jumped up out of bed and two of them ran down the hall stairs and into the kitchen. Caitlin cried out as she seen her mother forcing her father backwards over the kitchen sink. She was holding a butter knife in her hands, trying to stab Leon, who was using all his strength to keep the knife away from this throat.

"I'LL KILL YOU, YOU SON OF A BITCH!" Gerti was screaming, her face as red as her hair. Leon turned towards the cry of his daughter.

"GO GET HELP!" He yelled to her, still fighting to keep his wife from plunging the knife into his throat. As Caitlin ran down the front hall stairs, Stitch picked up where his sister left off and started screaming, hoping to keep his mother and father from fighting any more. He didn't dare go near them, but figured as long as he kept screaming someone would end it. It seemed like an eternity before Stitch heard the downstairs door slam shut. His Uncle Dan and Aunt Terri ran past him.

"GERTI!" Terri called out as she seen her sister-in-law trying to turn her brother into a shish kabob. Gerti kept her strength and with both hands tried to push the knife closer to her husband. Dan grabbed at the knife and told his sister-in-law to let go of it.

"I SAID LET GO!" Dan repeated, only louder.

"Gerti, let go of the knife."

"I'll KILL that BASTARD!" she screamed through clenched teeth.

"MOM NO!" Caitlin cried out.

"GERTI the KIDS!" Terri said again. "Oh my god!"

Gerti finally relented and allowed Dan to take the butter knife from her hands. Dan stopped and looked at the knife with puzzlement. "A butter knife?" he said. "What the hell were you trying to do, spread him to death?" He looked over at Gerti who was in the middle of the kitchen, bent over with her hands on her knees, trying to catch her breath. Leon was still bent backwards over the sink relieved it was finally over. As he stood straight, he caught Dan's eye and smirked. Dan began to laugh at the idea of a butter knife being used to attack someone. Gerti looked up with surprise and started to laugh as well. Caitlin looked at Stitch, who returned her look of curiosity as all four adults were now laughing. Suddenly, Gerti fell to her knees and began crying.

Terri rushed to Gerti's side and put an arm around her shoulder. "Gerti?" She asked, not sure what was wrong with her. "What the hell happened?"

Gerti told her in-laws how she spent the entire evening painting the living room and how he husband got drunk and started a fight, which led to him throwing his cup of coffee all over the new curtains and freshly painted walls. All her hard work and effort was suddenly reduced to stains of coffee. Everything she worked for on that night; to make thing for the better were nothing more than stained curtains. Dan looked at Leon and then slapped him in the back of the head. Leon just stood there, suddenly realizing what it was that he did. As time would pass, this would become known as the "Butter Knife Incident", or as Uncle Dan referred to it – the "Shiv Incident". Life went on, but not as usual for the LeRue family. Gerti worked in the Home and she had Leon at home with her as well. However, money was becoming tight, and bills were getting harder to pay. Belts had to be tightened and budgets needed to be followed if this family was to make it from one month to the next. Social Security Disability was paying Leon every month, but it was nowhere near what he was making as a machinist, not to mention that the check came only once a month. It was difficult trying to adjust their spending and plan for the entire month, rather than from week to week. Their financial crisis was starting to show.

Stitch needed new sneakers for school. His old "Keds" were worn down and beat up. The soles were peeling back and the small label on the ankle was completely gone. His mother had come back from shopping and told him she picked up his new shoes. When she pulled them out of the bag, Stitch felt his jaw drop to the floor. "What are those?" he asked as he stared at the blue and white vinyl shoes.

"They're your tennis shoes." His mother replied as she tossed them to him. "Don't you like 'em?" she asked.

Stitch knew he'd better watch his words; he didn't need to upset his mother. "Uhm, sure." He said as he looked over the shoes. The soles were yellow and felt hard, not like the soft rubber soles on Converse or Pro-Keds. The new shoes had soles that were real hard, like dress shoes; except they weren't black, they were blue with three white stripes on the sides, running from the laces to the soles. He looked up and forced a smile. "Where, uhm... where did you get them?" he asked quizzically. He asked in a manner that anyone could tell he didn't really want to know the answer. He had hoped to hear 'Cramer's Armory' or 'Sears', but something deep inside feared he was going to hear 'Fisherman's' or something ending in 'Mart'!

"I got them at K-Mart." His mother replied. She couldn't hear her son cringe, because he did it internally. All the kids at school were wearing Pro-Keds, or Converse, and some of them were wearing the newer shoes like Nike, and Puma. But Stitch realized those were too expensive for his family now. However, he also knew that he'd catch hell in gym class. "They're just like what Starsky, on '*Starsky & Hutch*' wears!" His mother said with a smile. "All the kids will be wearing them soon."

He made his smile go wide and thanked his mother. What she didn't realize is that, even though these shoes were blue with the same type of stripes as 'Starky's' shoes, they were not the same brand. These shoes were vinyl, not cloth. They had plastic soles, not rubber, running soles. He walked away and brought his new tennis shoes upstairs and placed them in his closet. *She's Clueless!* He though to himself.

The next morning, as Stitch was leaving for school, his mother handed him his lunch when she suddenly noticed his feet. He was still wearing the old, ripped, and dirty Pro-Keds. "Where are your new shoes?" she asked.

"Uhm..." He tried to think of a good answer. At 13-years-old, he'd gotten pretty good at coming up with stories. "I Don't have gym today, and I wanted to wait until gym class to wear them."

His mother looked at his feet and could see the toes of his socks, through the canvas of his shoes. "No." she said plainly. "Not at all. You march right up those stairs and you change those tennis shoes and throw those things away." She said while pointing to the stairs.

"But mom..."

"No buts about it, young man. Get rid of those filthy things."

Stitch reluctantly walked up the stairs with his head hanging in defeat. There was no arguing with his mother and he knew this. Once in his room, he plopped down on this bed, and kicked off his Keds and slipped on his K-Mart, blue light specials. Mentally, he prepared himself for what was about to happen. But it was futile. He knew there was no preparation for the day he was about to have.

As Stitch walked to school, he kept turning around, looking to see if someone was following him. He kept hearing footsteps, and then realized that it was his own. His old shoes never made a sound, but now he could hear the 'clip-clap' of the hard plastic soles on the ground. *Oh, great!* he thought to himself. He tried to walk softer, and perhaps a little slower. It helped some, but not by much. He was still making noises.

When Stitch got to the school, he still had twenty-five minutes before the first bell to homeroom. He stopped at "The Wall", where the rest of the students stood. He walked up to his best friend, Jared and bummed a cigarette from him.

"Why Don't you get your own?" Jared asked, as Stitch gestured for a light. "Can't you spare seventy-five cents for a pack of smokes?"

"If I had seventy-five cents, Don't you think I would have bought my own pack? Stitch replied. "Besides, if my mother found cigarettes on me, she'd kill me."

"Yer such a puss!" Jared said with a laugh as he reached out and flicked Stitch on the tip of his nose with his middle finger. Just then Jared's face became serious, as he looked past his friend. Stitch turned around and seen Benny Starks, walking down the path towards where they were standing at the Wall. The wall was the east side of the building, near the Shop Class entrance. It was out of the sight of the front office window and students generally hung there to smoke. It was also where many students went to find someone who was selling pot. Benny Starks was one of those salesmen that many of the "HEADS" would look for. No longer was school a place where kids stood in circles and told funny stories or played odd games like in grammer school. Now school was a place where young people were split into classes and cliques. The Jocks were the athletes in the school. The Prissies, were the Cheerleaders. There were also the HEADS who were individuals that partied every weekend. They met in the woods with a keg of beer and nickel bag of pot; drinking and smoking to oblivion. There were preppies, which could be jocks, but dressed like young adults. There were also Geeks, who were the weaker of the categories. They didn't do drugs, nor did they participate in sports, but their academic record was impeccable. There were also Freaks, who were in a category all their own. Some "Freaks" played sports, but got picked on by the jocks. Some "Freaks" did pot, but were messed with by the "Heads". Anyone else who didn't fall into any of these categories, were "Norms"; just your average, everyday, normal kid. Stitch and Jared were Norms, although Jared acted like he wanted to be with the HEADS, which is why the two of them would stand by the wall and smoke cigarettes. If the HEADS thought they were part of them, they would get invited to the HEAD banging parties and get wasted with the best of the HEADS. When Benny showed up at the wall, he nodded to Jared. It was more like an acknowledgement than a greeting, but Jared took it as an omen!

"Did you see that?" Jared said with enthusiasm.

"What?" Stitch wasn't sure what just happened, but clearly it was important to Jared.

"Benny just said, 'HEY' to me!" Stitch watched Benny lean back against the wall and light a cigarette and put one foot up on the wall, beneath him. Jared did the same, trying to be just as cool."

"So." Stitch said, not realizing he had just deflated the situation for Jared. "Big deal."

"Whaddya mean, big deal?" Jared said defensively. "If I can get in with Benny, I'll be invited to all the bitchin' parties."

Stitch waved him off and finished his cigarette. "You got any gum?" He said, holding out his hand. "I have Mr. Weiment for Homeroom and if he smells smoke on me, he'll give me hell."

Jared handed Stitch the gum. Just as he popped it into his mouth, the bell rang, signaling it was time to get to homeroom.

The day started out normally. The only thing different was the addition of a new student. His name was Gil Clarke and he moved to the Albany area from Johnstown. He was quiet and he kept to himself for the most part. Stitch sat in the back of the classroom with Derrick Dodson where the two would sit in the back and talk about the radio disk jockey they heard that morning on WTRY. Stitch would imitate the DJ when he recalled some of the skits from the show. Derrick would always laugh and tell Stitch he should be a DJ. Over the din of the classroom chatter, Mr. Weiment was calling attendance and the students were casually replying to the calls looking up from doing their last minute homework or catching a few extra "Z's" before first period.

"LeRue." Mr. Weiment said without looking up from his roll call roster. However, Stitch had his back turned to front of the room as he was still chattering with Derrick. "Mr. LeRue?" The teacher said louder, with a touch of annoyance. However, Stitch was still goofing off with Derrick. His eyes were closed as he imitated the DJ and he could not see the look on Derrick's face that would have warned him that Mr. Weiment was standing right behind him. The teacher leaned in close to Stitch and nearly yelled, "MISTER LERUE!"

Stitch literally jumped out of his chair as he spun around and looked up at his teacher with surprise.

"Do I have your attention now, Mr. LeRue?" He said sarcastically.

"Yes." Stitch replied. He was infuriated on the inside, but tried not to let it show.

All the classes went well, except for the fact that the new kid was in all of Stitch's classes. At the start of each period, the teacher would have Gil stand up and talk about where he came from, what his name is, and what school he attended before moving to Cohoes. You would think that he would get sick of saying it over and over, but he seemed to take pleasure in it. When Gil would stand up, Stitch would glance over at Jared, or Derrick or Dave and gesture his finger in his throat, as if he were gagging himself. Fortunately, gym class was coming up and coach Ed wouldn't care about such matters and no one would have to hear it again.

Stitch was pleased when Coach Ed sent the boys out onto the floor after he called attendance. The boys set up for relay races. The 'Jocks' of the class were picked to be the team captains of the relay teams, by Coach Ed. The rest of the class was told to stand against the wall and wait to be called upon by the team captains. Stitch hated this part of gym class because he knew that he would be called on last, or next to last. Myron Shulritz was always called last, and that gave Stitch a small boost to his ego since no one *ever* wanted Myron on their team. However, Stitch slumped as he noticed Myron sitting on the bleachers. Apparently, he had a note from his mother requesting that Myron be excused from gym for the next two weeks due to an ingrown toenail! Stitch wasn't very athletic; in fact, he was very skinny and sort of uncoordinated. He hated the fact that he was not the athletic type. Playing baseball with this brother and cousins was one thing, but having to perform athletically in front of his gym peers was another.

The captains made their picks and Stitch found himself still against the wall with the other "Freaks and Geeks" of his gym glass. He leaned back, with his foot resting against the wall, and under him as he bit at his fingernails while the captains called the boys around him. As he stared up at the ropes, which hung from the ceilings, the elbow of the kid next to him jolted Stitch.

"Dave called you." The kid said to him. Stitch couldn't believe that he was picked and there were actually several boys left against the wall. He jogged over to Dave's team and stood behind the rest of the boys. They all had their Cohoes Middle School gym shirts tied around their heads, or tucked into their shorts like a bandanna.

Stitch's shirt was clinging to his torso, and hanging outside of his shorts. Some of the boys had armpit hair or even chest hairs, where as Stitch was still covered in peach fuzz. As the rest of the boys groaned about the limited selection to choose from, Coach Ed lined up the teams and explained the race. Each member of the teams would have to run down the length of the gym, race around the last cone, grab a soft ball from a bag, hanging from the rope and then race the ball back to their team and drop it into a bin. The first team to fill their bin would win. Stitch looked up the rope and seen the bags hanging half way between the floor and the ceiling. He was never a very good rope climber and shuddered at the idea of having to do so. Coach Ed blew his whistle and the first leg of each team darted down the length of the gym. Carl, the kid on Stitch's team, took an early lead and ran around his cones like a snake, which serpentines through the trees of a forest. The gym echoed with the quick, rapid squeaks of the boys' tennis shoes as they stopped and started around the cones. Suddenly, Stitch became very nervous. He looked down at his vinyl shoes and groaned as he realized that he wasn't wearing his Pro-Keds. "GREAT!" he cursed to himself. Stitch had been picked third, rather than last. He didn't want to disappoint his team. If he did, he would go right back to being picked last for relay events, or any events! Carl jumped down from the rope with the ball in his hand. All the boys were cheering for their runners, but Carl was in the lead. He darted back through the cones, squeaking tennis shoes and all and jumped across the line as he slam-dunked the softball into the bin. Terry McClutcheon ran out and started his run down the gym. Stitch grew nervous, as he was in the next leg and would need to keep his team's lead. As Terry flew up the gym, darting in and out of the cones, the other teams were dropping their softballs into the bin, causing their second leg to take off. The captains were shouting, "C'MON! LET's GO!" All the boys were cheering for their runners to run faster and move quicker. As Terry was running back down the gym, Stitch's captain tapped him on the shoulder and gave him the thumbs up. Butterflies invaded Stitch's stomach as he pretended to warm up by bouncing on his toes. Terry arrived and slammed the softball into the bin, signaling Stitch to take off. His team had a healthy lead, and Stitch thought if he took it light, he wouldn't mess up their chance for a win. However, as he ran towards his first cone, Stitch felt his shoes slip and slide out from under him. The hard plastic soles of the tennis shoes couldn't get a grip of the finely polished boards of the gym floor. Stitch struggled to keep on his feet and then darted for the next cone, slipping as he rounded the cone and falling on his chest and face. He heard the boys behind him laugh and howl. However, his own team was yelling for him to hurry up. This continued for the next three cones. Stitch had to slow up to keep from falling and take wide turns around the cones. When he got to the rope, he jumped up and tried to use his feet to get a grip of the rope. His hands struggled to pull his weight, but his feet kept slipping as he tried to push up. He fought harder and harder to climb. Even with his Pro-Keds, he had a hard time with rope climbing. But now that he was wearing the 'Blue-Light Specials', he was having an even harder time than normal and it was starting to show. Stitch felt his neck and ears burn hot with embarrassment as he struggled to get up the rope. Coach Ed stood at the bottom of his rope, screaming at him to move faster and get to the bag. Stitch couldn't hold his weight any longer and slid down the rope, burning his hands. He looked at his team's angry faces and tried again to make it up the rope. He fought with all his might and mustered up as much energy as he could. He noticed the third leg of the other teams dropping their soft balls into their bins and the fourth legs coming out. Stitch was still struggling but finally made it to the bag. He jumped down to the floor and felt the sting of his weight pierce the balls of his feet as he hit the floor from the seven-foot jump. He hobbled back through the cones and dropped his softball into the bin and went to the back of the line where he dropped down without facing his team. "Hey LERUE!" Called Dave, his team captain. "Where the hell did you get those cheap ass shoes, K-Mart?" Dave nudged a friend and everyone laughed at Stitch's expense. The worst part of it was Dave meant it to be a joke, but it was true. They were K-Mart, blue light bin shoes and Stitch could barely stand on the gym floor with them. It was the equivalent of trying to stand on ice with tap shoes. Stitch brought his knees to his chest and buried his face into his legs.

"Kids can be so cruel." The woman said as Steven stood up from the floor and smiled. "You were a geek in school?" He said with disbelief. Steven was amazed by the story because Stitch stood more than six feet tall and was as big as Stone Cold Steve Austin, the wrestler. "You look like you could have beat them all up!" Steven said. "Why didn't you?"

"When I was younger, I was very small." Stitch said. "I was tall, but I was real thin and I was always afraid of confrontations." Stitch turned his eyes up to the boy's Aunt and realized he should probably say something to keep the boy from thinking confrontations were the answer. "Besides, fighting isn't always the answer."

"Teasing and fighting are always wrong." The woman said to her nephew.

"But I get teased every day, at school." Steven told his Aunt with a sad tone. Stitch noticed this visibly upset Steven's Aunt. She stood up from the sofa and shook her arms to calm herself.

"Then maybe you should tell an adult, or maybe one of your teachers." She said as she walked over to Steven and took a breath to calm herself down. Stitch was confused by how upset the woman was getting by the subject matter. He knew first hand that kids could be dick-heads, but it was nothing that could hurt anyone. Not more than hurting feelings, so he thought.

"Kids will be kids." Stitch said. But the woman shot him a look that should have turned him to stone. Stitch sat back in the chair and remained quiet as he let the aunt confer with her nephew.

"Never, ever, ever let anyone pick on you, do you understand?" She said to Steven as she swooped him up in a hug. "And if they do pick on you, tell someone, don't ignore it and do not fight over it."

"Yes ma'am." The boy said.

Stitch smiled as the boy referred to his aunt as *ma'am*. It took a lot of discipline for a child to refer to his elders as *sir* or *ma'am*.

"Did you ever get into a fight, when you were in school?" The young boy suddenly asked Stitch.

"Well…" Stitch started, but then looked to the aunt, not knowing how to answer the child. "I, uhm… I wasn't much for fighting when I was in school." Stitch said. "As a matter of fact, I was a bit of a pacifist when it came to fighting." Stitch sat back and took a large drink from his glass as he prepared to tell the young man another story.

"But even a pacifist can reach a breaking point." The woman smiled, and nodded from across the living room, letting Stitch know it was ok to tell him another story - almost as if she knew what the story was. Steven put his video controller down and turned around to listen to the large, bald man tell his story...

CHAPTER FOUR

April 7th 1977

"If I learned anything from my mother, it was how to fight". Stitch said as he started the next story. "Most guys would say their father taught them to fight, but for me, it was mom and even though the lesson was direct, she never stood toe-to-toe with me in the back yard to teach me how to bob and weave. My mother took a more practical approach and actually paid someone to teach her son to fight". Stitch stopped and re-worded his previous statement. "Well, actually she paid someone to beat me up"!

It was spring and the snow was mostly melted away. Stosh shoveled the last of the snow from the basketball court at Craner Park. Whenever he had the chance to throw basketballs, Stosh took it. With the air warm and the sun shining, Stosh didn't want to wait for the snow to melt so he did his part to move it out of his way. Stitch, Arnold, and Earl were on the other half of the basketball court, tossing a kick ball at a broken basketball hoop. There was no net and the hoop was bent downward and hanging from a few rusted screws. Their half of the court was covered with tiny patches of melting ice and small puddles of muddy water. Stitch and Arnold would try to splash one another with the ball as they passed it back and forth, while Earl would try to sneak in and steal the ball. Every now and again, Earl would succeed and Arnold and Stitch would chase after him. However, Arnold started complaining about his thumb hurting and took a seat on the concrete bench along the side of the court. As the two boys took a break on the bench, Earl watched Stosh dribble and shoot the basketball into the hoop on the one side of the court and then would imitate the moves with his kickball on his side of the court. Stitch and Arnold watched Earl and giggled as Stitch's little brother struggled to jump up and put the ball through the hoop. Arnold was becoming Stitch's best friend, as the two of them were spending a lot of time together. Arnold used to live on Front Street, which is right around the corner from where Stitch lived. When Stitch was younger, Arnold and he would play "pickle" with Stitch's cousins Vince and Stosh. The game is set up to have runners run between two bases without getting tagged out. It was easy to do if you could time it right. However, Arnold would just run. He didn't care who had the ball. If he was chased, he would simply dodge out of the way and then jump up into the air and land on the base directly on his knees. Stitch would cringe every time Arnold would do this, as the play area was in the middle of the road. Landing on Asphalt with one's knees was not the easiest way to land on the base, which normally was just a flattened piece of cardboard. Stitches used to think that because Arnold was Korean, he could do all these fancy martial arts moves and not get hurt. The fact of the matter was that Arnold was just a hyper little kid who thought it was funny to freak everyone out with his jumping. But Arnold moved away for a few years and when his mother got a job in the mills as a seamstress, they moved back to Front Street. This is when the boys started hanging out more and more. Arnold was a few years younger than Stitch, but they would do everything together. And when Jared would come down to visit with Stitch, the three of them were always together, never apart. Having Jared and Arnold around was as common to Stitch as having a left arm and a right arm and he felt just as helpless without one or the other. However, on days like this, when It was just Arnold and Stitch, they would mainly sit and talk about things they liked or disliked. As Earl was imitating Stosh's basketballs skills, Arnold and Stitch were talking about their favorite television shows, The Six Million-Dollar Man and Kung Fu; they started to imagine what it would be like to be as strong as Steve Austin or as fast as Kwai Chang Caine. Ironically, whenever the boys would play and pretend to be their favorite character, Arnold would pick being the Bionic Man and Stitch would have to be Caine. He always felt funny about that because he wanted to use his "Chinese" accent, but he didn't want to offend Arnold. Even though Arnold wasn't Chinese, he thought speaking in that manner would be offensive. It wasn't as if Arnold had an accent. He spoke just like everyone else, but his mother had a thick, Korean accent and Stitch thought he might make Arnold mad if he tried to talk in that manner. However, Arnold would always enunciate his words and be dramatic when he spoke as Colonel Steve Austin. He would place his hands on his hips; squint his eyes and talk as though we were reading from a comic book. It was fun for the boys and on this day, the water puddles on the basketball court were actually floodwaters coming forward on a destructive path towards the City of Cohoes. They imagined that they were summoned to create some kind of dam to keep the floodwaters from destroying their city. Stitch, a.k.a. Caine, came up with the idea of knocking over the Benchley Building and causing a temporary damn until the rains receded. In reality, he was talking about the park bench. It was made of concrete and posed a real challenge to both of the boys. Stitch and Arnold started rocking and pushing the bench, trying to get the pyramid style legs to tip all the way over. As the two boys tried, one of the other neighborhood kids showed up. John Macerelli. His family lived at the first end of the building that Arnold lived in. He asked the two boys what they were doing. Being a little embarrassed to say that they were playing 'Bionic Man' and 'Kung-Fu', Stitch just shrugged his shoulders. Had Johnny been anyone else, they probably would have said what they were doing, but Johnny was sort of like the neighborhood bully. He didn't go around beating people up, but he didn't have control of his temper. He would fight someone for no reason at all. Today, Stitch would find that out.

"C'mon Caine!' Arnold said, pretending to be the Bionic Man, Colonel Steve Austin. "We need to stop the flooding."

"Ah em doing da best dat ah ken." Stitch replied, taking a chance and speaking in the manner that Caine spoke. Arnold stopped and looked at his friend with annoyance.

"What the hell was that?" he asked defensively.

Stitch shrugged his shoulders and pretended he didn't know what Arnold was talking about. "What?" This was precisely what he was afraid of. He thought if he spoke in that manner he'd make Arnold upset and now he was sure he'd done so.

"da best ah ken?" Arnold mocked. "What is that supposed to mean?"

"It means 'the best I can', but the way that Caine says it." Stitch stopped trying to rock the bench and stood up straight. He was always afraid this would happen, and now he didn't know if he had just lost his friend or not.

"That sounded nothing like Caine." Arnold said. "It's like this." Arnold repeated back Stitch's words in a

Korean accent. Instead of imitating Caine, Arnold was actually imitating his mother. But Stitch couldn't tell the difference. It sounded great to him. "Hah! I am do-ING my BEST, hoy!" Arnold stood up proud. "It's supposed to be like that."

"What are you girls doing?" John asked, appearing out of nowhere. Embarrassed, Stitch thought John might have overheard the two of them imitating Caine.

"Nuthin'" Stitch said as he slowly took a seat on the bench. He knew Johnny would give him a hard time if he told him what they were really doing. But Stitch couldn't stop Arnold from talking.

"We're trying to tip over this bench." Arnold said. Stitch was glad he left off the Bionic Man part. "You wanna help?" Arnold asked.

"Uhm.. I'm sure he doesn't want to help us with something as silly as that." Stitch said nervously, trying to get Johnny to leave so the two of them could go back to playing again.

"Actually," Johnny said with an evil smile. "I'd really like to do that."

"OK!" Arnold said with joy. "Who do you wanna be?"

"What?" Johnny was confused by the question.

"You wanna be Steve Austin, or Caine?" Arnold asked. He was a few years younger than Stitch, and could get away with asking silly questions like that. When Johnny looked at Stitch for confirmation, Stitch just shrugged nervously.

"Little kids." Stitch said with a smile. "They say the silliest things, eh?"

Johnny ignored the question and moved to the side of the bench and grabbed the back and the seat at the same time. "I'll get on this side, and you get in the back." He said to Stitch, pointing to a spot behind the bench. Arnold moved to the other end of the bench seat and the three of them started rocking the bench. It was starting to go over, but then it suddenly fell back with a heavy thud and water splashed everywhere from under the large legs of the park bench. The three boys jumped back and laughed with excitement. Actually, only two of them laughed. Johnny stood there looking down at the muddy water on his trousers and sneakers. "Look what you DID!" he exclaimed.

"Sorry about that, man." Stitch said, still laughing.

"Sorry?" Johnny asked with annoyance.

Stitch stopped laughing when he noticed a touch of anger in the boy's voice. "It was an accident, man. I'm sorry."

Before this goes any further, let me bring you back in time another two hours. *Johnny was sitting with his brother and another neighborhood kid, across the street from Stitch's house. They were talking about a TV commercial they had seen, where a dog came trotting out talking about kibbles and bits. The boys were laughing at how funny it was when suddenly, a woman's voice called out to Johnny. "Hey, Macerelli."*

Johnny looked over to see Mrs. LeRue leaning out the second floor window. "Yeah?" He asked as he got up and walked across the street. It wasn't uncommon for the adults in the neighborhood to ask kids to run to the corner store for them. Kids loved doing this because most times, the adults let the kids keep the change. This was especially good when they gave you a five-dollar bill and asked for a bottle of soda or a loaf of bread. Johnny spotted a couple of green papers in the woman's hand and thought she was about to ask him to run to the store.

"I was wondering if you would do me a favor." She said in a lower voice. She waved the boy over to the spot under the window. When he got close enough to hear her, she explained what it was that she wanted. "I need you to do something for me."

"You need something from the store, Mrs. LeRue?" Johnny asked, placing his hands over his eyes, to block out the sun as he looked up to the second floor.

"Actually, I was hoping that you could do me a favor and get into a fight with my son."

"What?"

"I'll pay you!" She added.

"Naw..." he said, brushing the request away with a bit of laugh. "I can't do that." Johnny was sure she was joking

"Yeah you can." She said a little louder. She lowered her voice again when she realized how loud she'd gotten. "You don't have to hurt him, just give him a boost to his confidence. You know, roll around on the ground, push him around get him to fight back."

"I can't do that." Johnny repeated. But when he turned around to leave, he heard the sound of coins hitting the ground. Johnny turned around to see a few green bills floating to the Earth in front of him. "Mrs. LeRue, I'm serious..." he started.

"But I already paid you." Gerti said with a wink. As she closed the window she yelled one last thing. "Don't hurt him. Just give him a good scare."

Johnny reluctantly scooped up the money and then started looking around for Stitch. After all, he just made five dollars and he didn't even have to really fight the kid. All he had to do was push him around and scare him a little, how hard could that be?

As Johnny looked up from his pants, he ran towards Stitch and gave him a huge shove, knocking Stitch on his butt and into a puddle. Earl and Arnold froze in fear as they watched Stitch scramble to his feet. It was like watching something from the Wild Kingdom animal show, where a gazelle is knocked down by a jaguar and is fighting to get up and run. You know the gazelle is going down again and you know it'll be dragged off to a tree limb to be consumed by the jaguar, but you still have some hope for the little, horned gazelle. In the split second that Stitch took to get to his feet, Stitch suddenly had a million thoughts running through his head. *Will Stosh come over and stop this before it gets out of hand? Will Earl run to the house to get mom so she can stop this? Will it hurt real bad to get a fist in the face?* All these things occupied Stitch's mind so much that he barely noticed Johnny rushing toward him again. By the time he did notice it, the ground came up and slammed Stitch in the back of the head and Johnny was on top of him grabbing at his T-Shirt and pushing in on his chest. "LOOK WHAT YOU DID TO MY PANTS!" Johnny kept yelling. Stitch couldn't believe this was getting so crazy over a little dirty water on jeans. The worst part of it was that Johnny was getting even more water on his clothes by rolling around in the mud with Stitch.

"WELL LOOK AT MINE, MAN!" Stitch yelled back. He had nothing to lose now. He was already at the point of no return. He was angry and he knew he needed to use this anger to help him survive this. Fear gnawed at his insides as he tried to think of how to turn this around. If he could just show Johnny that he wasn't afraid of him, then perhaps Johnny would stop this. Stitch reached up and grabbed Johnny by the shoulders and pushed with all his might. He pushed off with his left leg and spun his body, knocking Johnny into a nearby slush puddle. But instead of hitting Johnny in the face, or kicking him while he was down, Stitch got up and ran backwards, while pointing at Johnny. "DON'T DO THIS, MAN!" Stitch said. He didn't want to hurt Johnny. That's all that he kept thinking. *If I hurt him, he'll hurt me back.* Johnny got up from the puddle with an evil smile on his face and ran towards Stitch, who sidestepped the kid. As Stitch looked around, he noticed that all the kids in the park were circling around them. "FIGHT, FIGHT, FIGHT!" They chanted. Stitch looked around and with pleading eyes he glanced at Stosh for some help. However, Stosh was chanting along with the rest of the kids. Then a familiar face showed up and it was Stitch's Uncle Greg. Stitch suddenly felt relieved, until he noticed his own uncle chanting along with the rest of the kids. "C'mon Stitch!" he said as he balled up his fist. "HIT 'EM!" Stitch felt helpless. He was hoping that his Uncle would get him out of this jam, but instead, he cheered him along. Stitch looked at Johnny and was about to charge ahead and tackle him. "*NO*!" was the only word that ran through Stitch's head. Stitch relented and turned on his heel and then ran as fast as he could from the park. As he jumped over the fence, he felt the embarrassment of running away from the fight and it stung worse than any punch could every sting. Stitch ran across Mohawk street and into his back yard. He threw open the back door and ran up the back stairs and straight up to the third floor and into his bedroom. He dropped to his knees and hid in the corner, crying and sobbing. The tears streamed down his face as he thought about how he could never face his friends again. After a while, his father came into his room.

"What's up, junior?" he asked as he knelt down next to his son. "Why are you crying?"

Stitch didn't answer. He slowed his breathing and tried to hold back his sobs, but the tears kept coming. After a few moments, Leon reached over and rubbed the hair on his son's head and told him not to be afraid of running.

"It takes a real man to walk way from a fight." Leon said softly. "Only that person with fear is the one who fights." Leon stood up and took a step but stopped at the door. "The real hero knows when *not* to fight."

After his Father left his room, Stitch sat back against the wall and let out a breath. His sobs had stopped and his tears were drying. He wiped the last of the salty water from his eyes and stood up to look out his window. Arnold and Earl and some of the other neighborhood kids were playing pickle in the road with Stosh and Vince. Across the street, sitting on Stosh's porch was Johnny. Stitch was tempted to step away from the window but Johnny looked up and caught his eye. Stitch froze, expecting his rival to flip him the finger, or to make a slashing motion across this neck. Instead, Johnny did something that Stitch never expected. He gave Stitch a "thumbs up" and smiled.

"It's weird." Stitch said as Steven sat on the floor, listening to the older man's story. "But I've never talked about that fight in all these years. I guess I carried that shame around with me all this time."

"You mean I'm the first person you ever told this to?" Steven asked. His face was intense and his eyes sparkled as he stared at Stitch.

"Yes." Stitch said with a smile. "You're the first person I've ever told that story to." Stitch took a drink of the water and then smiled. "Johnny and I never spoke about that again. But I was never afraid of Johnny after that."

"You see." Steven's Aunt said as she reached out and touched the boy's shoulder, to get his attention. "Fighting isn't always the answer."

Stitch sat and watched Steven finish his game. As he stared at the television screen and watched the gory images of a woman destroying zombies, his mind went back to a time when he was in Middle School...

MAY 13th, 1977

It was Friday the 13th and Stitch's day wasn't going well. Stitch's parents were having trouble balancing their budget. Getting a paycheck once a month was strenuous on the family of six and it was starting to show. The kids needed new clothes since they were growing so fast; and putting food on the table, paying utility bills and rent left little money to purchase clothes. However, Stitch's mom had read of a charity organization called "Cloth-A-Child". This charity donated $50.00 to each child and then took the kids shopping for clothing. The kids were able to pick out their own clothes and the first thing that Stitch picked out was a pair of Black Pro-Keds. He then picked out two pair of jeans and a few silk shirts. It was the time of disco and silk shirts were the "IN" thing. After the spring break, Stitch returned to school wearing his new cloths. He was happy to be wearing sneakers that would squeak on the floor again, and keep him from slipping and sliding on the high gloss floor. As Stitch put his jacket in his locker, Dave walked by and said, "Nice clothes, Stitch!"

"Thanks!" Stitch said with a smile. But then he heard those words play again in his head and there was definitely sarcasm in Dave's voice. Stitch turned to see Dave walking down the hall and snickering with a couple other jocks. As Stitch walked into his classroom, he could have sworn that he had heard snickering by his classmates. "Hey CUTIE!" one of the girls said. Stitch didn't need to hear that play back in his head again, since he knew that "CUTIE" was their sarcastic way of saying someone was ugly, or looked like a dork. Stitch couldn't figure this out. He wasn't wearing the K-Mart, Blue-Light special shoes anymore, he had his KEDS and... *"Maybe the silk shirt is too much."* He thought to himself. As he sat down in his seat, Jared glanced over at him and frowned. Stitch didn't know what to say.

"Yo, man." Jared said. "Do you know how many people in this school actually read the news paper?"

"No." Stitch replied. "Why?" Jared tossed a folded newspaper onto Stitch's desk and pointed to an article circled by pen. Stitch started reading. As his eyes scrolled across the newspaper, Stitch felt the back of his neck getting hot. The more he read, the more crimson his face and ears became. Stitch wanted to crawl into a hole and never come out. Apparently, his mother had written a letter to the local newspaper, telling them about the charity that put clothes on her kids' backs. All the kids in the school had read the article and everyone knew that he got his clothes from a charity. Rather than write the letter anonymously, she had gone ahead and used their names and listed the things that her children had purchased. "No wonder Dave was being such an asshole!" Stitch said as he tossed the paper back on Jared's desk. Since the jocks were always reading the sports section of the paper, to keep up with scores and statistics, Dave would pick up a newspaper every morning and bring it to class so he and the rest of his 'jock' friends could check out their favorite players' and teams' stats. Why couldn't they have just purchased the sports section? Why did they have to read the 'puff piece' on the front page?

After homeroom, Stitch went into English class and took his usual seat, in the back of the room. Sitting directly in front of him was Gil Clarke, the new kid. Even though he'd been in the school for almost a year, he was still referred to as 'The New Kid' until someone ever newer arrived. As Stitch opened his book to the assignment that was chalked on the black board, Gil Clarke leaned back in his seat and stretched. As he did so, his clenched fist smacked Stitch in the side of the head. Even though it was purely accidental, Stitch suddenly became infuriated. He'd had enough insult for the day and he knew he needed to respond. In his mind, the kid jumping the fence and running across Mohawk Street needed to stop running. He knew he had to stand up for himself. Stitch immediately reached up and slapped Clarke in the side of the head with a loud 'Thwack'. "Watch what the hell yer doin'!" Stitch said. But as Gil recoiled Stitch jumped up in case the boy retaliated. "HEY!" Clark said loudly. "Knock it off, you friggin' WUSS!"

Most thirteen-year-olds, can take a lot, but for everything that had happened to him, Stitch reached his stress level. With Dave's smart-ass comment, and Jared showing him the newspaper article, and now Gil Clarke (of all people) giving him the business, Stitch *knew* he had to stand up for himself.

"What did you call me?" He said though clenched teeth.

"I said you're a WUSS!" Clarke replied as he stood up from his seat. Stitch was a good head taller than the boy but was much skinnier and scrawny. "What are *you* gonna do about it?"

Stitch knew better than to do anything in the school, but the entire classroom was looking at the two of them standing there, toe to toe and nose to forehead. Stitch took a breath and said the words he'd heard many times, but never before uttered. "I'll meet you on the path, after school, fucker." Stitch said with a look of dead seriousness. He could feel the butterflies in his stomach and he knew he was taking a chance, but he felt it was something he had to do. He wouldn't back down from a fight this time. He was going to follow through with it. He knew his father told him that the smarter and stronger person walked away from a fight. So Stitch hoped that Gil Clarke would be the stronger, smarter person in this case. As the entire classroom "*Ooooo'd*" in response to Stitch's challenge, Mrs. Mitchell walked into the room.

She noticed the two students standing toe to toe and asked, "What's going on in here."

"Nuthin, Mrs. Mitchell." Stitch said as he slowly sat down in his seat, never taking his eyes off Gil's. Mrs. Mitchell walked to the front of the classroom and placed her books on her desk.

"Then take your seats." She said as she opened the attendance roster. The class slowly turned their attention back to the front of the class, but Stitch could hear the sarcastic snickers and whispers of his classmates. Some of them turned their heads to look in his direction, as they whispered to their neighbors, and chuckled into their hands. "*Stitch the dork just picked a fight with the new kid.*" Was probably what they were saying and laughing about. But Stitch didn't care what they thought. He was going to see this through and prove to himself that he could stand up and show that he was a man of his word.

During lunch, Stitch sat with Jared and ate his school-cooked lunch. His parents enrolled him in the "FREE LUNCH PROGRAM" because they were now considered low-income and he qualified for lunch tickets. Every week he needed to walk down to the principle's office and pick up the meal tickets. Each morning, his mother would place the tickets on the refrigerator with an alphabet magnet and remind him to take one, before leaving for school. It was a good program, but it was the High School equivalent of Food Stamps for Stitch and he was actually embarrassed about using them.

Jared was rolling his cheese sticks into balls and actually bouncing them off the tabletop.

"Can you believe this crap"? Jared said as he bounced a glob of cheese into the air but Stitch wasn't paying attention. He was focusing on a group of kids at another table who were playing tabletop hockey with a penny and their fingers. Jared held up his slice of pizza and let the grease drip off onto his tray. "Are you even listening to me"? Jared asked as he waved his hand in front of Stitch's face.

"What?" Stitch came back to reality.

"I said this grease is almost as nasty as Marge Collington's hair"! Jared made a face of disgust. Marge Collington was the one girl in the school that all the kids picked on. Even the freaks and geeks gave her a hard time. Ever since elementary school she had been a very heavy girl with greasy, brown hair and pimples. Stitch glanced over in her direction and seen that she was, once again, sitting alone and eating from a brown paper bag. She kept her hair covering most of her face and never looked up at the rest of the kids. Her gaze remained steadfast on her lunch before her. As Stitch brought his eyes back around to face Jared, he noticed Elaine Shannon pointing in his direction. A few more girls from her table were turning to look in the direction she was pointing. When they caught Stitch's eye, they quickly turned around and laughed. "HIM?" They squealed with laughter. "Oh MY GOD!" They gasped as Stitch's face turned red.

"What's wrong?" Jared asked as he stuffed the pizza into his mouth.

"Nothing." Stitch replied as he pushed peas around his tray with his plastic fork.

"You're not worried about that Clarke guy, are you?" Jared asked. Pizza grease began running out of the corner of his mouth and he used his hand to wipe it back.

Stitch was a bit surprised by the fact that Jared had heard about it. "Who told you about that?" Stitch asked.

"Are you kidding?" Jared took a swallow of milk. "It's all over the school! Everyone is going to be there to watch you guys fight."

"Aww man!" Stitch couldn't believe that word of his pending duel had spread so fast. He was pretty sure that he could take Gil Clarke, but what if he couldn't. What if this kid whooped his ass in front of the entire school? He'd have to move away and go to a new school district. He couldn't handle having to deal with the shame of getting his ass beat by the new kid.

"Stitch." Jared said as he swallowed his glob of cheese. "You're not worried about this joker, are you?"

Stitch shrugged his shoulders. "Not really." He said as he stared at his tray. "I'm more afraid of everyone else."

Without thinking, Jared started speaking. "I hear he knows Karate."

Stitch sat up with a bit of nervousness. "What?"

Realizing what he said, Jared twitched in his seat. "Well, you know..." He had no idea where to go with this. "He's probably just bluffing. You know, trying to scare you."

Stitch shook his head in defeat and pushed his tray away. "I'm not hungry."

It was 2:58 PM and Stitch kept looking at the clock. Gil wasn't in his last period and he was hoping that the kid ran off early. Stitch would walk out to the path and wait for the kid. If he didn't show up, Stitch's status would not change. He would still be the dork who gets his clothes from charities. However, if the new kid did show up, Stitch would have to beat him. If he didn't, he would be worse off than just the dork. He would be the pitiful dork who got his ass beat by the newer dork. If he did beat the kid, his status might just jump up a touch. Stitch glanced up just as the minute hand clicked over the number twelve and suddenly the bell rang. Stitch's stomach flip-flopped and fluttered under his 'QUEEN' T-Shirt. The room emptied out and Stitch walked out with the rest of the kids. However, as he thought he was following the crowd, he soon realized that a crowd was following him. Stitch strolled through the main doors and walked out to the path. As he walked, he could hear the students talking behind him. Some of them muttered that they heard Stitch knew karate. Others said that it was the new kid who knew karate. Stitch was getting sick of this and picked up his pace. As he reached the path, he noticed the rest of the school was standing there waiting for him to arrive. He felt like a Roman Gladiator as he strolled into the center of the mob. It was as if they were Romans surrounding him in the coliseum while the leaders and senators were watching from above. Stitch glanced up on the roof of the metal shop annex and seen a few 'Heads' smoking cigarettes and looking on. Stitch just stood there, holding his jacket and his books at his side. Soon the din of the surrounding students calmed as Gil Clarke came around the bend and showed up. Stitch's butterflies became worse. He didn't know how to begin. Should he just rush up on Clarke and start punching the shit out of him? Perhaps try to talk him into an apology and shake on it? *Nah that would never work.* He thought to himself.

When Gil arrived, he came to a stop and just stood in front of Stitch, who dropped his books and jacket with dramatic flare and held his arms out to his side as if to say, "What's up?" He looked Gil in the eyes and seen fear and in some sick sense that made Stitch feel better.

"You better think again." Gil said as he trembled and pointed a finger at Stitch. "I know Karate and I really don't want to hurt you." Now Stitch knew how Johnny felt when he rolled around on the basketball court with him. Johnny must have sensed fear in Stitch's eyes because Gil was acting just the way Stitch acted all those years ago.

Stitch was feeling brave, having seen the fear in the new kid's eyes. He chuckled and said, "Bring it on, man."

"I'm serious, man!" Clark cried out in desperation. He was almost in tears and this made Stitch feel even better about his situation.

Stitch raised his fists up and took a step towards Gil. As he moved in, Gil raised his foot and tried to complete a round house maneuver but he was too slow. Stitch slapped the kid's foot out of the way and then, with his other hand, he slapped Gil in the face with a stiff back-hand. Gil fell to the ground and the crowd around them "*ooo'd*" in unison like the crowd at a fourth of July fireworks display. Gil quickly got up and dramatically stomped his left foot down as he spun around and swung out his right foot and made a karate yell. "Eey YAH!" However, Stitch just slapped the kid's foot out the way again; stepped in and with a closed fist and for the first time in his life he punched someone in the face. Gil's face spun around and he fell to the dirt. Again the crowd made an exclamation as Gil's head bounced off the path. Gil quickly jumped up and did the same thing. Stitch couldn't help but laugh at the kid as he maneuvered around the kid's foot again and once again punched him right in the face, but only harder this time. Gil's head went backwards and again he fell to the ground. However, Stitch wanted to end this, so he quickly jumped on Gil and straddled his chest and started punching him in the face. Each time his fist hit Gil's face; it only made a dull thud. He didn't hear the loud 'CRACK' like the sound effects in the movies when people fight. So Stitch hit him harder and harder as he tried to reproduce that sound. After all, Stitch wasn't sure when he'd be in a fight again, and he wanted to make sure he did everything just right for this one. Stitch's arms were working like the pistons of a car engine as they wracked against Gil's face and head.

Suddenly a hand out and pulled at Stitch's shoulder. It was a girl from Stitch's class. "STOP IT!" She screamed. "You're gonna kill him!" Stitch was surprised by the genuine concern in her voice. She was a 'Head' and Stitch thought someone like her would have enjoyed seeing such a spectacle. But Stitch took her advice and stopped punching the boy's face. He stood up gasping and stepped back from Gil's limp and battered body. Stitch couldn't believe how exhausted he was from fighting. He expected Gil to curl up into a ball and cry, but the boy just lay there with blood pouring from his nose and a cut above his left eyebrow. Suddenly Stitch could feel his knuckles throbbing and he realized his breathing was heavier than ever. He regarded his victim for a moment until he felt Jared at his side.

"C'mon, man." Jared said as he came out of nowhere. "I think you've done enough here."

The crowd around them was silent, which was a severe contrast to Stitch's heavy breathing and pounding heart. Stitch walked past Dave and a couple other jocks and picked up his jacket and books. He wanted to say something to them, but didn't know what to say. Before he left, he turned around to Gil's direction and for some reason, Stitch felt the need to finalize the fight by screaming, "Who's the friggin' WUSS now?" He didn't mean to scream so loud and sound so psychotic, but adrenaline was still pumping through his veins and his knees were knocking together. Gil didn't answer him. He just lay in the dirt, holding his face and crying. As Stitch walked down the path with Jared, leaving the crowd behind, he couldn't help but feel sympathy for Gil. He was the new kid and now he was beaten silly in front of the entire student body. Part of Stitch felt bad for the boy, however, another part of him felt proud that he was able to stand up to the challenge. In Stitch's mind, he could see Johnny giving him the thumbs up again.

Stitch and Jared walked out to the main road together and neither of them said anything about the fight. Stitch smiled as he realized what a good friend he had in Jared. The two had been friends since the second grade and it looked as though they would be inseparable. Deep down, both boys knew just how traumatic an event that fight had been for Stitch and both boys appreciated each other as they walked home from school in silence.

CHAPTER FIVE

Steven finished his game and turned it off before sliding the entire console under the television stand. As he finished, he turned and asked Stitch a question that brought forth a memory that Stitch had nearly forgotten. "Were you a bad kid, or a good kid?"

Stitch smiled as he contemplated the question. "Was I a *bad* kid?" Stitch repeated as a way to stall for some time. He knew he was no angel, but he didn't want to share that with too many people. He smiled and asked, "What do you consider *bad*?"

"You know, like - did you ever do stuff that made your mom punish you?"

Stitch laughed out loud. "I did plenty for my mother to punish me." He said. "One time me and bunch of kids skipped school. We thought if we switched jackets, no one would know who we were. Except we were all hanging out together and when a friend's mother seen us she knew who exactly who we were because of our jacket! Regardless of who was wearing them. I got in a ton of trouble with my father when he got word of what I did."

"Your mom didn't punish you?" Steven asked.

"My mother was visiting her sister in California when that happened." Stitch replied. "If she was there, I wouldn't be sitting here today." Stitch smiled but that comment made Steven curious.

"You were more afraid of your mom?" He asked.

"Let's just say the punishment was always justified, but I never looked forward to it when it came from my mother." Stitch looked up and caught the woman's eye. She was smiling as she watched her nephew listen to the man's stories. If Stitch didn't know any better, he would swear that she was enjoying the stories as well.

JUNE 12th, 1977

Stitch and his family were driving back from his Aunt's house where they went to a pool party. His father's sister had moved to Watervliet and purchased a house with a pool. For her open house, she invited all the family and told them to bring their swimming trunks. That evening, after the party, as they drove down the back road from Watervliet to Cohoes, they passed by St. Coleman's Home. A shiver went up Stitch's back as he looked at the large, dome shaped building. Apparently, it was a home for children who were bad and needed to be taught a lesson. At least that is what his mother and his Uncle Greg would tell Stitch and his siblings about that place. Gerti's belief was that if the kids were afraid of St. Coleman's, she could use it as a type of threat to keep her kids in check, so she and her brother Greg would tell Stitch and Earl horror stories about that place. One story in particular that Stitch never forgot was how they kept children locked up in a basement and fed them only scraps of food; and If they were real bad, they would get chained to the walls and have toothpicks shoved under their fingernails. The very thought of all that made Stitch cringe as they drove by the place.

"There's St. Coleman's Home, kids!" Gerti said as she pointed out the window in the direction of the building. It wasn't her intention to sound morbid and dark as she pointed out the building; it just came out that way and it struck a nerve with all the kids in the car.

Stitch and Caitlin shared looks of horror as they sat quiet and didn't dare move out of line because they believed if they did, they would be delivered to the doors of St. Coleman's Home for the *Troubled and Wayward Children*.

There were many times when Caitlin and Stitch would fight and argue or get into mischief and Stitch's mother would threaten them with being sent to St. Coleman's home. Stitch's first memory of this was when he was very young. He snuck into his sister's room and took her lipstick and ate it. To him, the lipstick not only looked like candy but it smelled like candy as well. He knew he was doing wrong by eating his *sister's* 'candy', but he didn't realize he was doing wrong by eating her lipstick. Caitlin was only three, but the "pretend" make-up kit had "actual" make-up in it! Who the hell gives a three-year-old real lipstick and make up as a gift? Could you really blame four-year-old Stitch from eating it? Caitlin cried and Stitch's mother caught him red handed, (*literally*). Stitch's deep blue eyes contrasted the dark red lipstick that covered his face and hands. He thought he was going to be yelled at for eating his sister's candy, but instead, his mother laughed at her little boy with the painted red face and hands. As Stitch smiled, his mother's laugh dimmed and she became serious as she threatened him with those words -- *"Do you wanna go to St Coleman's home, young man?"* Stitch stared at his mother; and unfamiliar with those words he became scared.

"That's where they put bold little boys and girls." she said to him, trying to make him see how being a "bold boy" would not be advisable. "Do you want to go there with all the other bold boys and girls and have nothing to eat except for bugs and dirt?" Stitch's eyes grew wide and shined like sapphires. Being only four-years-old, this story was very scary. His mother smiled at him and proceeded to wipe away the lipstick from his mouth and face.

For the next nine years Stitch and Caitlin heard all about St. Coleman's Home and the horrors that little children faced for their misdeeds. As they drove by it, Stitch and Caitlin starred at it, big as life. As the sun set over the edge of the hills, it cast an eerie shadow over the dome-shaped structure. It looked like a giant soccer ball that was half buried in the Earth. There were swing sets, monkey bars, and slides in what appeared to be a play area. When Stitch asked why there was a play area for bold girls and boys, Gerti said it was for their visiting family. Both Caitlin and Stitch looked over at Earl to see the familiar look of horror brought on by the mention of St. Coleman's Home. It made for a quiet ride home. The children didn't make a peep. They just sat in the car and listened to the radio broadcast of the Red Sox double-header game against the Texas Rangers as they rode home with Uncle Danny and Aunt Terri. Danielle looked at the three of them as if they were nuts. She knew St. Coleman's Home was just an orphanage, but she said nothing. She also knew that if she said anything to Stitch or Caitlin, her Aunt Gerti would not be too happy and Danielle knew better than to make Aunt Gerti anything other than happy.

Once everyone was home and Earl and the baby were put to sleep, Caitlin and Stitch were allowed to stay up a half an hour later. Stitch always felt proud to be the oldest because he was able to stay up the latest. The baby was put to bed at 8:00, then Earl to bed at 8:30, followed by Caitlin at 9:00 and finally Stitch went to bed at 9:30. In that half an hour before going to bed, he would sit up with his mother or his father and watch television with them. He felt as though he was an adult just as they were and he reveled in it. As Caitlin and Earl would go off to bed, they would always exclaim, "Why does *he* get to stay up?" As always, Stitch's father would reply back, "*When you're his age, you can stay up that late too. Until then, GET TO BED!*" Caitlin would pout as she stomped her angry feet up the stairs to her bedroom. Stitch looked up at the ceiling as he heard her feet stomp across the floor, all the way to her bed. When the next thirty minutes flew by, Stitch's father made a gesture with his thumb, like a hitchhiker and told Stitch that it was time for him to 'hit the sack'. Stitch got up and gave his mother a kiss and a hug goodnight. Then he approached his father and was about to give him a kiss and hug but his father pulled back. Stitch's heart nearly stopped.

"What?" Stitch asked with sad eyes.

"You're twelve-years-old." Leon said. "Boys your age don't kiss their fathers, they shake hands."

Stitch turned to look at his mother, who was sitting on the end of the sofa with her feet curled up behind her. He wanted confirmation on this information since he'd never heard of this law before. Gerti gave her husband an angry look. "Kiss your friggin' son!" she said.

"Boys don't kiss their fathers." Leon shot back. "It's just not right."

"What's not right about it?" Gerti challenged.

Stitch stood in the middle and looked back and forth between the two as they argued as if he were at a tennis match. Leon struggled to find a logical answer that he could articulate, but all he could come up with was one answer. "It's just not right, ok?" Leon put his hand out for Stitch to shake so Stitch relented and shrugged his shoulders in defeat. He took his father's hand and started shaking it and then, quickly pulled his father's hand up to his mouth and kissed it.

"GOTCHA!" Stitch exclaimed as he bolted out of the living room and ran through the kitchen.

"You little son-of-a-bitch!" Leon yelled as his son disappeared into the kitchen. He looked at his wife and found her laughing hysterically. "You think he's funny?" Leon asked as he crossed his legs and grabbed a cigarette from the table next to his chair.

`"No." Gerti replied as she fought back the laughter. "But I think you're pretty damned funny!"

Leon lit his cigarette and took in a large drag before he turned back to Gerti. "What's so funny about it?" he said, as the smoke rolled out of his mouth and nose.

"He's your son, you friggin' idiot." She replied.

"That's right. He's a teen-age boy and I'm his father."

"So?" Gerti couldn't see where Leon was going with this.

"So!" He flicked an ash into the ashtray. "So I don't want him growing up to be a queer."

Gerti's mouth went slack and her green eyes grew wide. "You think you're son is going to be queer if he kisses his father?"

Leon thought about the question. "What if he grows to like kissing men, huh?" He retaliated. "Then he'll always want to kiss men."

Gerti shook her head as if feeling sorry for her husband. "You are a goddamned idiot." Gerti replied with deadpan expression."

Little did either of them realize that Stitch was standing outside the living room door, in the hallway from the kitchen, listening to their argument. Stitch smiled at his father's naivety. He knew he wouldn't like boys like that. He was already interested in girls and had no desire to be '*that way*'. However, it did hurt Stitch to think that his own father didn't love him enough to show affection. Stitch went quietly up the stairs and carried out the same routine with the lights since he still feared the little munchkin demons and didn't dare chance it. After all, if it worked this well for the past four years, why stop now?

The next day at school, the principle announced over the loud speaker that the middle school students would be going home two hours earlier than usual. Apparently, the teachers and school staff had a meeting of some sort. As the bell rang, all the students rose up from their seats and ran to their lockers and headed out the doors. Stitch threw all his books and papers into his locker and bolted out the back entrance of the school, onto the large soccer field. As Stitch ran across the field he noticed his brother and sister's school was still in session.

"HA!" He yelled out loud. "YOU GUYS STILL HAVE SCHOOL!" Stitch exclaimed at the top of his lungs. He wanted the students of the elementary school to know that the older kids were off and already on their way home. He didn't know why, but he felt that he needed them to know it. He ran closer to the school and yelled again. "WE'RE OUT OF SCHOOL," he yelled out in a sing-song fashion. "YOU GUYS ARE NOT!" As Stitch got closer to the school, he noticed that the back doors were opened and he smiled an evil smile to himself. He started running as fast as he could, heading for the back doors of the elementary school. As he crossed the threshold of the doors, he yelled at the top of his lungs, "SUCKERS!" and bolted down the long hallway, laughing as he listened to his word echo in the long, narrow corridor. His Pro-Keds were squeaking as he turned the corner and headed for the front door of the school. "YOU'RE ALL STUCK IN SCHOOL!!" And then he broke through the front doors and headed down the street towards the main road that he would take home. He laughed the entire way and stopped at the bottom of the hill as he caught his breath. Stitch had ran so fast through the school, he wasn't even sure if anyone had noticed him because he surely didn't notice anyone else. He'd kept his eyes focused on the front doors and kept his feet moving the whole time. It was amazing and the adrenaline that rushed through his body was like a sugar blast from drinking an entire pitcher of Kool-Aid! *Too bad Arnold or Jared couldn't have been here with me*. He thought to himself. He imagined it would have been so much more exciting with his friends to share in it with him.

Stitch was filled with exhilaration and sat on a bus stop bench as he reveled in his memory of what he had just done. Never before, in all his life, had he done something like that. Suddenly, he grew a little sad that no one would know what he'd done. Once he'd caught his breath, he started walking again. He decided to take his time walking home. After all, he had two hours to kill. His parents didn't know that school let out early for him, so they weren't expecting him home so soon. Stitch decided to take the long way home and walked the railroad tracks. He picked up a piece of timber and a handful of large rocks, which were all over the tracks. He imagined he was number 72, Carlton Fisk, of the Boston Red Sox as he tossed a rock up in front of him and then bashed it with the piece of timber. The sound of the rock banging off the wood made a loud *KNOCK* and echoed off the walls of the paper mills. Stitch imagined it was game six of the '75 World Series and he had just hit the home run that brought the Bo-Sox to victory. He cheered himself and pretended to be the announcer. "*PUDGE had just hit the game winning home run*!" Stitch pretended to run the bases, just as Pudge had done in the 1975 World Series. Stitch remembered how that game looked as the ball sailed over left field and bounced off the left field foul pole. At first it looked like it would be a foul ball, but then it bounced in bounds and the fans went crazy. Stitch imagined that the Boston Red Sox players were lifting him up and cheering him. He replayed that memory all the way down the tracks, hitting rock, after rock, after rock. When he finally arrived to the point where he needed to get off the tracks, a part of him grew sad that it was over. He hit one more rock and watched it sail down the tracks and then dropped his timber and proceeded home. As he jumped over the fence, he noticed his hands were covered in oil from the railroad timber and the rocks. He spit on his hands and rubbed them together and then wiped them onto his jeans. His hands were now clean, but his mother would kill him if she couldn't get the oil out of his jeans. Stitch walked into the kitchen door and peeked into the living room to see if his parents were home. He noticed his mother sitting on the sofa folding clothes. When he turned towards the refrigerator to get something to drink he heard something that made him grow cold on the inside. "Leon Tyler LeRue Junior". His mother said calmly from the living room. Stitch froze when he heard his mother use his birth name *and* his middle name AND JUNIOR.

"Oh crap." Stitch said to himself. He tried to think of what he might have done wrong. He remembered cleaning his room, his cigarettes were hidden behind a loose brick, on the side of the house and he wasn't late for school that morning. He wondered what it could have been. "Me?" he asked innocently as he tried to buy time to figure out what was happening.

"Is there any other Leon Tyler LeRue Junior in this house?" His mother asked with a hint of sarcasm. She knew to use the 'Junior' because one other time she called to him and when she asked, "Is there any other Leon Tyler LeRue in this house?" Stitch smiled like a little smart ass and replied, "Duh! That's Dad's name ya' know." He got smacked for being such a wise ass, but it was laughed at later.

Stitch closed the refrigerator door and calmly walked into the living room. Uncle Tim was sitting in the recliner and smiling at him. However, it wasn't a friendly smile and it gave Stitch the creeps. Ever since Uncle Tim scared him, that one night, he didn't trust the man.

"How was school, today?" His mother asked with a mock smile. She batted her eyes dramatically, letting Stitch know that she knew something.

"Uhm, School was ok." Stitch replied nervously.

"Anything *special* happened today?" She asked. The emphasis on 'special' made Stitch more nervous.

Stitch pretended to think about the question before answering. "Not really." Stitch replied. "Why?"

"I received a phone call from Rosie." She said as she tossed the folded trousers up onto the back of the couch.

DAMNED! Stitch thought to himself. He had completely forgotten about the crossing guard at his kid sister's school. She was probably sitting right outside the doors of the elementary school and he went racing by too fast to notice her.

"Do you have anything you wanna say to me?" Gerti asked.

Stitch looked at her and then looked over at his Uncle Tim, who was smiling a wide, evil smile. Stitch tried to play it cool and pretend he had no idea what she was talking about, but he wasn't doing a very good job of it. His nervousness was starting to show through. "W..w..what did Rosie say?" Stitch asked with a quiver in his voice.

"She told me that you were running through your sister's school and screaming in the hallways." She said calmly. "Is this true?"

Stitch knew he had no way out of this, but instinct told him to LIE and DENIE! "No ma'am." He said politely. But his mother knew better. Stitch never uses ma'am unless he's trying to be the polite child who *needed* to look innocent.

Gerti decided to use her own version of parental psychology. She sat back on the sofa and grabbed another pair of trousers and started folding them.

"I see." She said while keeping her attention on the folding. Stitch was really nervous. He didn't know why he followed such silly impulses but it just seemed like innocent fun at the time. "Well just don't do it again." She said calmly. "Do you understand?"

Suddenly, Stitch realized that it was no big deal to his mother and that he wasn't in trouble at all. He sighed with relief and smiled. "Ok." He replied as he smiled with relief. "I won't do it again."

"AH-HA!" He mother said as she jumped up from the couch. "YOU LITTLE BASTARD!"

Stitch's heart nearly stopped as he realized that he'd been tricked and he'd stuck his foot right in his mouth. "I'M SORRY!" He yelled as he cowered away from her.

"Tim, get the keys to your car." She instructed. Stitch looked at his Uncle Tim as he got up from the chair and went to the kitchen. "YOU!" she said, pointing her finger at Stitch. "Go upstairs and pack your clothes." She handed him a garbage bag. "You can pack them in this."

Stitch reluctantly took the bag from his mother's hand but couldn't move. He stood there, twisting at the end of the plastic bag in a nervous manner. "Why... why do you want me to put my clothes in this?" He asked without looking up at her.

"Don't ask questions, just do it." Gerti was angry and fuming made, but Stitch was too scared to do anything. Part of him knew why he needed to pack his clothes, but another part of him wouldn't allow him to believe such a thing. It was too horrible to even think about.

Stitch took the garbage bag up the stairs and into his room. He slowly grabbed at one of his shirts from the dresser drawer and placed it into the bag. He paused for a moment, wondering if she would really do what he feared she would do. He tried to think of other scenarios that might be more logical for someone to have to pack their clothes. *Is she going to make me walk around naked?* He asked himself. He grabbed another shirt and put it into the bag when suddenly his mother came out of nowhere and snatched the bag from his hands.

"FASTER!" she said. "LIKE THIS!" In one motion she scooped out all his shirts and let them fall into the garbage bag and then opened the top drawer and scooped out his underwear and socks and stuffed them into the bag.

"Now get your pants and meet me downstairs!"

As his mother stormed out of the room, Stitch started putting things together in his mind and everything was coming up to confirm his worst fear. He was packing his clothes for a trip. His Uncle Tim was getting the car. He'd done something wrong and he was to be punished. *OH NO*! He thought to himself. Stitch grew nervous and finished stuffing his jeans into the garbage bag. He had a terrible feeling about everything and could only hope that he was wrong.

Stitch found his mother and Uncle Tim standing in the hallway at the top of the stairs waiting for him. He stood there as they waited for him, with his garbage bag of clothes slung over his shoulder like Santa Claus. "They're all packed." He said meekly.

"Let's go." He mother ordered as she started down the stairs. But she was stopped by his question.

"Uhm..." Stitch was almost afraid to ask, but he had to know. "Where are we going?"

Gerti stopped on the third step and looked straight into her son's eyes. "For some reason, you can't seem to stay out of trouble. No matter what your father and I try to do to correct you, it just doesn't work." She paused and looked away from him for a moment. When she brought her eyes back to his she said the words that he feared more than the munchkin demons. "I'm taking you to St. Coleman's Home."

Everything that Stitch had ever heard of that place suddenly flashed in his mind like a horror movie and he was the main character. Without even thinking, he screamed at the top of his lungs. "NO!" the sound echoed through the hallway and down the stairs. He took a step back from the stairs and dropped his garbage bag of clothes. "NO NO NO!!" he screamed while shaking his head. He couldn't believe that he was to be cast to such a dark, evil place. "I'll be good from now on." He bargained. "I PROMISE I'LL BE GOOD!" Tears flew from eyes and his body shook in fear. He couldn't imagine being chained to a wall. The very idea of having toothpicks shoved under his fingernails was sickening and was making his weak.

"LET'S GO NOW!" his mother said through gritted teeth. Gerti grabbed the garbage bag with one hand and reached for her son with the other. But Stitch stepped back and Gerti nearly fell forward on the steps. She grew angrier with the boy and shot forward with her hand and grabbed him by the collar of his shirt and pulled him towards the steps. "Don't make me any angrier than I already am!" She said through clenched teeth. Stitch stifled his cries and tried to muster the strength to obey his mother as she held him like a pet owner holds their pups by the scruff of their neck. Once she let go of his shirt collar, he reached down to grab his bag. He tried to convince himself that this was a scare tactic and that they would just drive by and he wouldn't have to actually go into the place. He followed his mother down the stairs and out onto the front stoop, where his Uncle

Tim was already waiting. Stitch noticed Arnold sitting on Vince's stoop with Stosh and some other neighborhood kids. Arnold was about to call to him, but when he seen the fear in Stitch's eyes, he decided against it. Gerti had a bit of a reputation in the neighborhood and the neighborhood kids knew better than to piss her off. But for Stitch's sake, Arnold knew better than to do or say anything that would make matters worse for his friend.

"Get in the fucking car!" His mother said as she opened the back door. But Stitch stood there, at the curb, petrified and afraid to get into the car. He looked over at the other boys with pleading eyes but they turned away. They too, were afraid of Stitch's mother when she was angry. Vince knew something was up so he waved to his aunt as he called out, "Hey Aunt Gerti." But Gerti just shot him a look and turned away. It wasn't anything personal, she was just very upset with Stitch; however Vince felt the chill and returned back to what he was doing.

"Can I say goodbye to my friends?" Stitch asked as a last request. But his mother refused and demanded that he get in the car or she would put him in the car herself. Not wanting to be thrown head first into the back seat, Stitch quickly obeyed. He slid over, behind the passenger side and his mother tossed his garbage bag of clothes into the backseat, next to him.

The drive was quiet. His mother didn't say a word and his Uncle just smoked a cigarette and flicked ashes out the window. Every once in a while, Stitch would catch his uncle looking as his mother and moving his mouth, as though they were whispering or mouthing something to one another. This didn't help the situation any. Stitch was being conspired against and it bothered him; especially since it was his Uncle Tim and his own mother doing the conspiring.

As the car turned down that familiar back road, Stitch grew more nervous. He could see the domed shaped building on the horizon over his mother's shoulder. He put his finger in his mouth and started gnawing on his fingernails. He felt his teeth *click* as they cut into the nail before he grabbed at the nail with his teeth and pulled at it. He could feel it tear across the top of his finger until he felt it pulling at the end. Stitch felt a sting as he tore the nail from the cuticle and a tear welt up in his eye as he noticed the salty taste of blood on his tongue. Stitch had done this to four of his fingers and both thumbs as they drove closer and closer to, what was in Stitch's mind, the most horrific building in the Capital District. Suddenly, the car turned down a road that Stitch was unfamiliar with. He sighed in relief as he thought this was all just a prank. But that relief was gone quicker than it had arrived. Stitch noticed it was the front entrance to the building and the car slowed down and came to stop. Uncle Tim didn't even turn off the engine.

"Get out." His mother said emotionless.

"What?" Stitch asked. He couldn't believe that she wouldn't even walk him up to the doors and say goodbye to him. "Right here?" He asked with tears in his eyes.

"Let's go!" His Uncle Tim said in a deep angry voice. "Get the hell out of my car." Stitch grabbed for his garbage bag and then looked to them again, hoping they would reconsider but that was not to be. "NOW!" Uncle Tim yelled.

Stitch quickly fumbled for the door release as he cried tears of fear and sadness. He pulled the bag from the car and closed the door. Just as he was about to approach his mother's window and beg for her to let him go back home, the car pulled away from the curb leaving Stitch alone and sobbing like a baby. At the very least, he wanted to hug his mother and say goodbye to her. He wanted to try one last time to plead to her that he would not be bold any longer. The car grew smaller as it slowly drove away from Stitch and left him standing alone in front of the St. Coleman's Home. Stitch cried louder and shook with fear which only worsened as he turned to face the hideous building that would now be his home; suddenly he noticed a nun, in full habit, coming down the walk and heading toward him. *HOLY CRAP, This is it!* He thought to himself. He suddenly recalled the stories his mother had told him and remembered how she said it was the Catholic Nuns who did all the horrible things to the bad children. Stitch's fear peaked as his legs began pumping like pistons and he started to run in place. He didn't know where to go or what to do, but he wanted to run. His legs were pumping up and down but he was going nowhere. Fear had gripped him and held him place. As he danced there screaming he heard something that caused him to open his eyes. It was at that moment when he'd seen his mother's face looking at him from the passenger side window of Uncle Tim's car.

"Get in the car." She said reaching back to open the door from the inside. Stitch immediately jumped in the car and pulled the garbage bag of clothes in behind him. The door slammed shut and Stitch's Uncle Tim pulled away from the curb. Stitch looked up to see his mother staring at him. He didn't know what brought her back to him and he really didn't care. All he cared about was the fact that they were driving away from that horrible building and the nun who was coming to take him away.

"I'm sorry!" He sobbed. "I'll be good from now on, I promise!" Tears were streaming down his reddened face and his hair was soaked from sweat and tears. Gerti said nothing as Stitch kept repeating himself over and over that he would no longer be trouble. The entire ride back home, he muttered these words, hoping that his mom would understand that he was serious in his promise.

When Stitch returned home, there were no more children playing outside and he was grateful for this as he did not want them to see him in the state of horror that he was currently in. Stitch grabbed his bag and was lugging it up the stairs when he noticed his father standing at the top of the steps.

"Where the hell have you guys been?" Leon asked. But Stitch didn't answer. He knew his mother would fill Leon in, so Stitch kept walking by, dragging the bag of clothes behind him.

"What's with the garbage bag?" Leon had gone for a walk before all the excitement and had no idea what had happened.

As Stitch got to the top of the bedroom stairs, he heard his mother talking to his father. He couldn't make out the words, but Stitch was pretty sure that she was explaining everything that happened.

"YOU TOOK HIM WHERE?" Leon yelled out loud, angry that she would do something like that.

As Stitch was putting his clothes back into his dresser his crying lessened. He knelt on the floor pulling out his jeans and re-folding them before placing them back into his dresser when he heard footsteps coming towards his door. Stitch looked up to see his father standing in his doorway.

"I guess that was pretty scary, huh?" Leon asked.

Stitch nodded, too ashamed to speak a word. He simply put his jeans in the drawer and then pulled out another pair and started folding them when Leon said something that brought Stitch to tears again.

"Are you all right?" was all he said. Apparently, it was all Stitch needed to hear to realize that his dad didn't' need to kiss him good night to show him love. Stitch jumped up from the floor and ran to his father, who knelt down to accept his son. Stitch threw his arms around his father's neck and exclaimed, "I won't be bad any-more, dad!" His father hugged him back and patted his shoulders.

"I know you won't." Leon said in calm voice. The two stayed embraced for nearly two minutes before Leon let his son go. He gripped Stitch by his arms and looked him in the eye, while on bended knee. "You're a good boy." He said. "You just have to remember that, okay?"

Stitch nodded as he wiped the tears from eyes and sniffed the snot back into his nose. "I will." He said softly.

Leon stood up and pointed at the bag. "You put your clothes away and relax for a while."

Stitch nodded and watched his father leave the room. He smiled as he recalled the argument his father had with his mother, about boys kissing their fathers. Stitch felt better to know that his father didn't want to be kissed, because he was concerned for his son, not because he didn't love him. As Stitch tried to remember, he could not recall one time that his father and he had embraced like they just did. Stitch knew his father loved him and from then on, whenever he said goodnight to his father, Stitch gave him a firm, solid handshake accompanied with a smile.

CHAPTER SIX

"That's so sad." The woman said as she sat back on her sofa and looked at Stitch with concern on her face. "Your father didn't want you to kiss him?"

"That's just the way he is." Stitch replied with a fake smile. He wanted her to think that he was okay with it, but deep down on the inside he really did wish his father had been more affectionate with him. "He was brought up that way and he just thought he was doing the right thing for me." Stitch realized that his father wasn't the most open person when it came to feelings and emotion. He recalled the time he went to visit his father in the hospital, after his eye surgery.

When Stitch explained to his principle that his father was in the hospital, Mr. Archibald granted young Stitch permission to leave a few hours early to visit with his father. Since the hospital was just up the road from the school, Stitch thought he would surprise his father with an impromptu visit. *That should cheer him up.* Stitch thought as he walked up Columbia Street towards the small hospital.

When Stitch approached the Cohoes Memorial Hospital, he wasn't sure which entrance to use. He noticed the emergency entrance and avoided it since it was marked for ambulances and emergency vehicles. Stitch looked for the main entrance where he entered and found an information desk. "I'm looking for my dad." He said to the elderly woman behind the desk. "He had eye surgery and I want to visit with him." Stitch smiled as the woman looked up at him over her bifocals as if he had just interrupted her tea time or something. She quickly licked her fingers and then scrolled through a file of index cards where she found his father's name and directed him to the appropriate wing of the small hospital. Stitch walked down the hallway as directed and felt proud that he was doing all of this on his own. He imagined the look on his father's face as he walked into his room and surprised him with a visit. He was sure that his father would be very appreciative of the visit and very proud of his son for taking the initiative for walking all the way to the hospital just to pay him a visit. Stitch couldn't contain his smile as he approached his father's room. However, before he could cross the threshold of the doorway, Stitch noticed his mother standing by the large window of his father's private room. She was looking out at the bare trees and gray clouds. Leon's bed was reclined up and he had bandages over both his eyes. The television was turned off and there was a small radio next to Leon's bed that was playing very low. Neither spoke. Leon just sat there, listening to the soft music coming from his radio and Gerti stood by the window looking out at the cold weather. Suddenly, Stitch's happiness faded as he observed his mother and father. They were not sharing in a conversation nor were they trying to reassure one another that everything would be okay. It was as if neither of them wanted to be there; like they gave up. Stitch slowly backed away from the door and walked back down the corridor towards the main entrance of the hospital. As he took his steps, he tried to fathom what would keep his mother and father so distant from one another. Neither showed the other any sign of love or appreciation. Both of them sat in silence seemingly tolerating one another.

This memory faded as Stitch looked at his watch and realized he had spent way too much time in the kind woman's house. He stood up from his chair and thanked both of them for their hospitality.

"I really appreciate you allowing me into your home." He said as he slowly walked from the living room to the doorway of the dining room. He sincerely did appreciate her hospitality and didn't know how he could ever repay her for what she'd done for him. He felt as though he had just spent hundreds of hours with a therapist. He glanced at his watch again. "Geesh" he said. "I've taken more than enough of your time, I apologize."

"No need to apologize." She said as she walked through the dining room and into the kitchen. She placed his glass in the sink after rinsing it out. The sense of familiarity struck Stitch again as he watched her move from the kitchen sink to the table where she sat down. He kept staring at her. "What is it?" She asked when she noticed his look of quandary.

"You never told me your name." The way he said it didn't make her believe that he was trying to ask a friendly question, but more like he was searching for something. She smiled as she leaned back in her chair and crossed her arms over in front of her.

"You mean you don't remember me?" She said coyly. "I certainly remember you."

Stitch's eyes grew wider as he studied her. He wondered if he went to High School with her and tried to place her face, but couldn't recall where he'd seen her. "We know each other?" Stitch was legitimately shocked by this. "I don't remember you."

"Are you sure?" She stood up and approached him. As she drew closer, he took a step back until he felt the counter at the small of his back and realized he couldn't move any further. She stood inches from him. "You told me how you went to Abram Lansing's School, and you don't remember me?" Her smile was coy.

Stitch tried to recall her face, but it had been more than thirty-years since he went to that school. He could barely even recall what his *teacher* looked like, let alone his classmates. "You went to Abram Lansing," he said accusingly. "Then who was our teacher?" He felt confident that she would not get the answer right as he was nearly positive that she was just pulling his chain. He didn't remember telling her any of his teacher's names from school, so only if she truly went there, could she be telling the truth.

"Mrs. Balstroak." She replied plainly; without even missing a beat. She didn't think of the name, nor did she stutter the name. It flowed from her lips as if she'd said that name a million times. Stitch was shocked and she smiled as she watched him try to figure out who she was. "Pretend I'm fatter." She said as she stepped back. But before Stitch could make a mental picture, she corrected herself. "No, wait!" she said with a smile. "Pretend I'm *LARGER*."

Stitch's eyes went wide and his jaw fell open. Immediately he remembered her. *'Large Marge'*. He knew better than to say that name out loud. He scrambled through his memories to recall her last name. "Marge Collington?" He said as he studied her closer. "Oh my god, is that really you?" Suddenly his smile faded and his face went flush. He felt as if the counter had turned into the large, hulking stove and warmed up the entire room. His embarrassment was showing and he knew that she could see it. Suddenly, Stitch was back in the schoolyard, running around on the playground, throwing rocks and sticks at an over weight, homely girl named Marge. Her hair was plain and hung straight in her face and down to the middle of her back. It was greasy and dirty and her breath always smelled like potato chips. Her clothes were always patched and dirty and boys would run away from her if she came too close while girls would pretend to be her friend, only to turn on her and make her cry. She was not like everyone else; she was different and everyone made sure to remind her of just how different she was. ***No wonder she became so upset when he nephew said he was picked on***. Stitch recalled.

Once Stitch's class reached Middle School, the pranks were crueler. The girls were more and more heartless, and her reaction to it was always more severe than the time before. Stitch recalled and incident where Marge was coming into the classroom and as she sat in her assigned seat, the girl who sat behind her held a pencil on Marge's seat. She wanted Marge to sit down on the pencil and get poked in the butt. She figured if she made Marge's life hell, the teacher would move Marge to another seat. However, the plan backfired when Marge sat down and the pencil didn't poke her in the butt. Stitch remembered he was sitting in the back of the class, doodling on a piece of paper when he suddenly heard someone cry out in agony. All the kids near Marge were laughing and pointing at her as she was writhing around on the floor. Stitch jumped up from his chair to see what all the excitement was about. However, the laughter soon turned into gasps of horror as the students noticed that the pencil was not in Marge's butt. Instead, it had penetrated her. That memory was new to Stitch as he had completely forgotten about that incident until that very moment while looking Marge in the face. The attractive woman that looked so familiar to him was the same '*Large Marge*' that writhed on the floor in English Class and had to be carted out by paramedics. He was speechless and it showed. He wanted to say something; to apologize for every cruel thing he ever did or said that offended or hurt her. Marge could see that he was struggling with his memories and his thoughts so she held up a hand with a mock smile.

"Please." She said plainly. "Don't even try to apologize."

Stitch could feel that his mouth was still hanging open and he slowly closed it. ***Where is she going with this?*** He thought to himself. His eyes darted to her hands, making sure she wasn't hiding a gun, or a butcher knife. When he noticed that he was safe for the moment, he looked into her eyes. He didn't know what to expect when he'd seen them. Pain? Anger? Either of these emotions would be justified.

"Since I moved back here, I've run into a lot of people from our class." She said without moving. "Some of them had no clue who I was at the time. Others remembered me immediately and the first thing they wanted to do was apologize." She smiled and moved back to the kitchen table and turned around to face him as she continued. "I understand that kids can be cruel. I was sort of an oddball, but that comes with the territory when you have six other siblings and your mother is a widow." She glanced at the tiled floor and then back to Stitch who was engrossed in her words. "My mother lived on food stamps, too. Only difference from your situation is that we looked forward to them." Stitch felt a twinge of embarrassment. "We tried to budget them because my mother couldn't work. When my father died, we had to live on what his life insurance gave us which wasn't much. We lived in a run down house, we had no car, and we had to wear clothes that our mother picked up from thrift stores or from the church. We didn't have access to some of the things that you talked about. The things that you were embarrassed of would have made our lives a hell of lot easier." Stitch's embarrassment grew like a wild fire. There he was, crying how terrible his life was, and she was listening to him talk about the things she would have given anything for.

"After my incident in Miss Ryan's English class, my mother was distraught. She blamed the incident on the fact that she couldn't work. Once I got out of the hospital, my mother moved us to Florida and we started over with the help and kindness of a family friend. She let us live in her home, bought us new clothes and helped find my mother a job so we could eventually live in our own place." Marge stopped for a moment and took a breath trying to settle herself. "So… so please, don't apologize, because in a way, that incident helped us more than it hurt us." She turned away from Stitch and looked out the window into the back alley. As she leaned her hands against the windowsill, she let her head hang. Stitch approached her from behind and placed a hand on her shoulder trying to offer comfort. Immediately she swung around and took a defensive posture. Stitch took several steps back and raised his hands to show he meant no harm or disrespect."

"Please, don't ever touch me." She said softly. "Especially if I can't see you."

"I'm sorry." Stitch said. "I'm sorry if I upset you, I just…" He didn't know what to say. He didn't want to give her pity because he knew that was the last thing she needed. "I just felt like you needed to know that I was still here."

"It's all right." She said, as she straightened her posture and became more relaxed. However, Stitch could tell that it wasn't all right. She let out a nervous laugh and shook her arms, as if trying to wiggle off a colony of ants. "I just get creeped out when I think of all of that."

"That's understandable." Stitch said as he kept his distance. "I always thought you moved away because Benny Starks put fire crackers on your window."

"You knew about that?" She said as she cocked her head.

"Yeah, it's all he talked about all that summer."

"And he said that *HE* put the firecrackers on my window?" Marge was visibly upset by this information.

"Well… Yeah. Didn't he?" Stitch didn't know what she was about to say, but ever since that day, Benny always claimed to be the reason that '*Large Marge*' left Cohoes. When Benny told his story, Stitch immediately thought of the movie "CARRIE", and imagined seeing an empty lot, where Marge's house should have been. Stitch had always compared Marge with the character in that movie. Other than their weight, the two girls were very similar in looks, appearance, and personality.

"Actually, I caught him peeking in my window at me, with Harry Guldmen." She said with a smile. "*I* threw the fire-crackers at them to scare them away, but the firecracker exploded against my window, instead of going out through the screen." She looked up at Stitch who was holding back a laugh. It was funny to him when he thought about Harry and Benny running away from a firecracker explosion. The image in his mind as the two 'tough guys' ran away from

Large Marge's bedroom window because of a tiny firecracker was funny to him and he could barely contain his laughter. Marge looked angry and he didn't know how to react to her story. "The window broke into pieces, ya know. And there was glass all over the place." She said, trying to show how serious the incident was. But Stitch couldn't hold it back any longer as he pictured the glass windowpane exploding and Benny running away. Stitch began to chuckle and eventually it turned into an outright laugh. Stitch noticed Marge starting to smile too, despite how serious she looked earlier. Soon, the both of them were in a full belly laugh. Stitch felt comfortable with Marge. His eyes were no longer searching for knives or guns. She was more pleasant again, as she was before he found out who she really was.

The two new friends relived old memories from School. She told him how the 'incident', (as she would refer to it), caused severe damage to her reproductive organs, and she could not have any children of her own. She spoke of how her sister got mixed up with the wrong people who lured her back to Cohoes, from Florida and got her mixed up in drugs, alcohol, and eventually she became pregnant. Marge explained how she moved back to Cohoes to help her sister. "I sometimes think I failed her." Marge said. Stitch reached across the table and offered his hand. He respected her wish not to be touched but felt it necessary to at least make the offer. She smiled and accepted his gesture. As he grasped her hand he explained how important it is that she understands that someone can't be helped unless they want to be helped. Something he knew all too well.

"Is there a story to that bit of advice?" she asked as she smiled. A single tear rolled down her cheek.

Stitch smiled. "There is another story." He said. But his smile faded. "But that's for another time." Stitch stood up from the table and thanked Marge for her hospitality.

"You never did say what brought you back to Cohoes." She said as she walked him to the kitchen door. "Why did you leave Pittsburgh to come back here?"

"Our Class Reunion." Stitch replied. "I came back so I could see who got fat and bald over all these years." He noticed her eyes look to the floor. "Didn't you know about it?" He asked.

"It was in the paper." She replied as she looked back to him. Her face was smiling, but her eyes were not. "But I didn't go to High School with you guys, so…" She let her statement hang there for a moment. Stitch started to smile. "What?" She wasn't sure what he was smiling about, but it was infectious. His blue eyes were sparkling and his smile grew wider. "WHAT?" She asked as she too started to smile.

"Marge Collington," Stitch said as he dramatically bowed before her. "It would be an honor if you would escort me to my class reunion." He said in an exaggerated cockney accent. He peeked up from his bow and noticed that her smile had faded. "What? What's wrong?" he asked, not sure if he just insulted her or not.

"I can't go to that thing." She replied. But Stitch could sense that there was more to it than just not wanting to go. "Those people made my life a living hell." The anger returned to her face. "Every morning that I woke up, I dreaded going to school and facing those kids." She paced a moment and Stitch suddenly regretted asking her to accompany him. "I was twelve-years-old and contemplating suicide one summer because I dreaded the idea of having to put up with the teasing and tormenting for another school year." Marge was on the verge of crying as her voice grew with anger. She put herself in check as she realized Steven may have heard her.

Stitch stood up and shoved his hands into his pockets as he shrugged his shoulders. "Are you telling me that you regret getting to know me?" He asked softly.

Marge couldn't comprehend what Stitch was trying to say. She looked at him as if he had carrots growing out of his eyes. "WHAT?"

"You knew exactly who I was when you invited me into your home." He said plainly.

"So?" She retorted.

"SO!" Stitch stepped closer to her and placed his hands out, inviting her to take them. "Even knowing that I was a creepy kid, who called you names, you opened yourself up to me, and now look at us." He smiled at her, getting her to smile a little as well. "I'd say were friends now, wouldn't you?"

"I guess." She smiled.

"You *GUESS*?" He threw his hands down over dramatically and pretended to be hurt by her words. "Oh you ***WOUND*** me!" He laughed as he noticed Marge laugh at his antics. "C'mon. Say you'll go with me."

"It's tempting." She said, now looking more like the woman who invited him up to see her apartment. "But I really can't. I have no one to sit with Steven, and besides, it's our night for movies, tonight."

Stitch conceded to her and playfully bowed to her again. "As you wish."

"But I wouldn't mind if you wanted to come back." She said, biting her bottom lip, and looking very shy. "You could tell me how it was; tell me who got fat, and who went bald." She laughed as she used his words to get him to smile.

"You bet." He said with a wink. He turned and walked down the steps to the front hall door. He stopped for a moment and looked at floorboards and then stared at the large, green door with the rusty number four screwed to the panel between the glass panes. With one last wave to Marge, he exited the building and made his way down the street before stopping to take one last look at the apartment windows on the second floor of number four Cataract Street. The frigid November breeze stung at Stitch's cheeks with the feel of winter in the air. Suddenly, his mind placed an image of a short, fat Christmas tree in the living room window and Stitch started to smile as he remembered all the Christmas Holidays…

DECEMBER 1976

Stitch used to love when his mother would bring out the Fake Tree on November 1st and make Leon put it up. November 1st was Leon's birthday and Gerti had the perfect gift for him each year. She would break out all the Christmas gear and lay it at his feet and make him put up the tree. Understand, this is just the day after Halloween when she would tell Leon he had to untangle all of the Christmas lights and toss tinsel. That would drive Leon NUTS! Then, just to make things worse for him, Gerti would ask the kids if they wanted to help. Of course! Little kids were always eager to help with putting up the tree and decorating it. However, Stitch, Earl and Caitlin were just little kids and didn't realize that Gerti was just torturing Leon for going out the night before and getting stone-cold drunk. The kids would get into everything and they would really piss Leon off; even more than Gerti had already done and Leon would curse Gerti's name the entire time he was working on the Christmas decoration. However, Gerti would always bitch right back at him.

"Be a fuckin' parent and do something with your kids, other than scream at them." Or she would tell him, "Fuck you, just deal with it!" the responses alternated back and forth each year."

Stitch, Earl and Caitlin were each sitting on the floor in front of the television screen while Melanie sat on Leon's lap in the chair behind them. Each of them had a small

Tupperware bowl of freshly popped popcorn and a tumbler of Kool-Aide. All the lights in the living room were out, except for the lights on the Christmas tree, which sat squarely in the middle of the living room window at the end of the sofa and fit perfectly into the corner. In front of three kids was the large, console style, floor model RCA Television that centered their family room. A ceramic Santa Claus sat on top of the television along side a set of rabbit ears antenna. Earl and Stitch sat on the floor with their legs crossed in front of them; however, Caitlin sat with her legs to her side and her feet pointing behind her. It was as if she thought about kneeling down and then immediately changed her mind and planted her butt between her feet; something Stitch could never get used to seeing. The kids had been waiting for weeks for the cartoon to start as they had seen the commercials for this cartoon for the past twelve days. Leon and Gerti loved it because they were able to use the cartoon as leverage, telling the kids things like, "*If you don't clean your room, you won't be able to watch Rudolph*." Finally, after weeks of being good and doing chores and not fighting with one another, the event had finally arrived and everything was perfect. That is, until Earl noticed that Caitlin's knees were too close to his "Zone" and he immediately slapped at her leg and told her to move over, but Caitlin, being who she truly was, gave Earl an evil look and said, "You move over, I was here first!" As the two argued, Stitch remained quiet as he knew what would be coming. He kept his mouth shut and observed while counting down in his head, *five.... four..... three.... two.... one...*

"KNOCK IT OFF!" Leon bellowed. Caitlin and Earl's heads spun backwards to argue their points with their father, but the look on Leon's face should have warned them that arguing wasn't a smart thing to do. However, Earl and Caitlin were too young to realize that look just yet.

"But she was touching me and..." Earl started to say.

"I was here FIRST!" Caitlin defended. The two went back and forth for almost a minute before Leon put an end to it.

"GO TO BED!" He said loudly. Caitlin and Earl immediately stopped and turned back to the television. Most parents would have been satisfied with the outcome, but to watch Leon, one would actually believe he enjoyed torturing the kids.

"Did you NOT hear me?" Leon said as he moved up to the edge of his chair. "GO TO BED NOW!" Melanie sat quietly on Leon's lap and didn't dare to budge.

Caitlin turned around and with huge crocodile tears as she proclaimed, "But Rudolph is coming on!" The whine in her voice was enough to make one believe that she was being abused.

"Are you going to be quiet?" Leon asked, indicating they had one more chance.

"We'll be good." Caitlin and Earl said unison.

Stitch suddenly noticed that his father was looking at him.

"Well?" Leon asked with an annoyed and cynical tone.

Stitch was confused by Leon's question. "What did I do?" he asked innocently. After all, he had only been sitting and watching is siblings argue and Stitch wasn't even in on it.

"Do you wanna go to bed right now, you little bastard?" Leon wanted to make sure that all of his children understood there would be no goofing off, but Stitch was practically insulted by the insinuation.

Not too many people would find this to be the "Special Holiday Memory" that one might expect, but to Stitch, this memory was the true holiday. His father may have cussed at them and things may have been less than stellar in their home, but it was all real and not the 'made up crap' that came across with television sitcom families. Leon didn't have a '*How to Raise Children*' guide to follow and even if he did, he wouldn't be able to read it very well. The man had to drop out of school in the sixth grade to get a job in order to help support his family, as did many of his older siblings. Leon knew what it was like to struggle as a kid and a young adult. Continuing to struggle as a parent really weighed heavy on him; and since he didn't know how to cope with it, he usually took it out on his kids by yelling. The worst part of all is that Stitch and his siblings didn't understand why Leon was the way he was. They didn't realize that his eyes often gave him pain that he couldn't treat. They didn't see him and Gerti worrying over the bills and pacing the floors to come up with a new corner to cut in order to make ends meet. They grew up thinking he was just thought a mean and grouchy person. They also failed to realize they were no angles.

Leon sat erect in his chair as he eyed his eldest son and warned him to keep quiet or he would have to go to bed. Most kids would just agree and say they understood and that would be the end of it. However, Stitch was not 'most kids'. He let it be known that he was not the culprit and was quite vocal about it.

"Dad! I wasn't doin' nuthin'!!" Stitch defended.

Fed up and frustrated, Leon gave up. "Alright, GO TO BED right now!" He said as he slapped his hand on the arm of his chair in an effort to drive his point across. Melanie's eyes blinked and her face contorted to the loud slam of Leon's strong hand against the thick, wooden arm of the chair. Stitch was confused by everything. Suddenly, in his mind he tried to find justification in Leon's actions but couldn't. After all, he was only watching and listening to Earl and Caitlin, how did everything get twisted around on him? Suddenly, it got to be too much for Stitch and he broke down into a teary cry.

"But...I....I...I wasn't doin' nuthin'!" Stitch cried out in a fit of rage. He was about to miss out on Rudolph because of his kid siblings and to him, it wasn't fair. He began feeling angry and betrayed. But Leon couldn't take it any longer and he just sat back in his chair and coldly said. "Then shut the hell up and watch the friggin show."

A few moments later, the commercial ended and the television screen faded to black. The room became dead silent as the screen slowly came to life with the image of the network logo... The 'Announcer Guy' said, "THE FOLLOWING IS A CBS SPECIAL PRESENTATION BROUGHT TO YOU IN LIVING COLOR!" The room soon lit up with the magical colors of the television as Stitch, Caitlin and Earl sat with a huge smile on their tiny faces, but their eyes were locked onto the large television screen just a few feet from away from those tiny faces. The 3-D animation was amazing for them; Stitch tried to figure out how they made the puppets move without wires. He realized it wasn't a cartoon like those he watched on Saturday Mornings. It was almost like a cartoon, but NOT quite. They were in awe. Earl sat still the entire time, transfixed on the television screen with eyes that sparkled like jewels as he never turned from the screen. Stitch, however, turned around to see how Melanie was enjoying the show, but she and Leon were fast asleep in the chair. Stitch quietly got the attention of Earl and Caitlin and pointed to their dad as he raised a finger to his lips, telling them they should be quiet. Stitch felt a little less on edge knowing his father was asleep. There was less of a chance of being scolded or sent to bed if Leon was sleeping.

As the show went on, Stitch reached into his bowl and ate popcorn and took of sips of Kool-Aid. He was finding it enjoyable to fill his mouth with a handful of popcorn kernels and then take a small sip of Kool-Aid and feel the fluffy kernels dissolve on his tongue. After a half dozen times of this, he noticed the popcorn was gone from his bowl and all that was left were a few un-popped kernels. Stitch watched the show and unknowingly grabbed at one of the kernels in his bowl and moved it around, making a path in the salt and butter. However, when Stitch tried to pick up the "Popcorn Seed" it shot out of his greasy, salty fingers and bounced off one of the tree ornaments. Everyone's heads snapped in that direction, including that of Leon. His eyes may have been going bad, but his hearing was impeccable!

"What the hell was that?" Leon asked in a groggy, sleepy voice, but the kids just shrugged their shoulders and replied in unison. "I dunno." Leon let it go and Stitch was relieved that he narrowly escaped getting into trouble again as he sighed relief and turned his attention back to the show. However, Stitch's brother knew exactly what happened; and he looked back at Leon whose eyes were fluttering as he succumbed to his fatigue. Once Leon had fallen back to sleep, Earl looked over Caitlin's head and whispered, "Do that again." The smile on Earl's face was priceless; causing Stitch to smile back as he picked up one of the popcorn seeds and squeezed it between his fingers again, but it didn't go anywhere. Stitch then realized he had to make the kernel slippery. He rubbed it in butter; at the bottom of his bowl, again. Slowly, he picked up the seed and this time, he aimed his fingers at the Christmas tree and... "PING!" He hit another ornament with a high velocity popcorn seed. Suddenly, Earl and Stitch noticed Leon's reflection in the silver, mirror-like ornaments as he sat up quickly and looked in the direction of the tree. The two boys could barely hold back their laughs. Suddenly, Stitch had an idea and immediately picked up another popcorn seed, smeared with butter, and waited for Leon to relax again. Just as he sat back in his chair, Stitch put the squeeze on the rock hard kernel and let another fly across the room and bounce off another ornament.

"WHAT THE FUCK IS THAT NOISE?!" Leon shouted as he sat up with real frustration at that point. Leon couldn't see anyone "throwing" anything and he didn't see the kids reacting to the noise each time he heard it, so he didn't know what to think. Stitch and Earl were in such hysterics that Earl had to bite at his hand to keep from laughing out loud. Stitch had to do the same things; he was laughing like a maniac on the inside but fought to keep looking like the perfect angle on the outside. He thought if he could hold out for just a few seconds longer he would have gotten away with it too, however.....

"It's Stitch!" Caitlin said, without taking her eyes from the television. "He's flinging popcorn seeds at the tree."

Stitch was SO PISSED off! He knew what his dad's reaction would be, so he did what any kid his age would do when backed against the wall... "Nuh-Uh! It ain't ME!" he lied.

"Well if it's not you, then who is it?" Leon asked

"I dunno, but it ain't me." Stitch said with a little too much innocence.

"Yes you DID!" Caitlin spit her words like venom as she turned her attention towards Stitch. "You almost hit me with one of em; it zinged right past my nose!"

Stitch just sat on the living room floor as he tried to force a surprised look on his face. He thought hard and realized he needed his dad to think he was telling the truth while making him to think that Caitlin was the liar and then Leon would send her to bed rather than Stitch. As Stitch did his best to think of the perfect tale to turn things around for him, Earl chimed in and said, "Yes you were, Stitch; don't lie."

"Alright, I've had it. Go to bed, right now." Leon said as he only wanted the night to end and for the kids to finally go to bed. "I'm sick of all this bickering!"

"But dad..." Stitch started to say, but was quickly cut-off.

"I don't wanna hear your friggin' excuses!" Leon said, letting Stitch know that his time was up by pointing to the ceiling. "Go to bed now, or I'll beat your friggin' ass!"

Stitch was pissed off! In his mind, he was being punished while Caitlin and Earl got to stay up and watch the rest of the television show. Stitch took a page from Caitlin's book and stomped his feel as he stormed out, through the Kitchen and headed to the stairs. He stomped his feet on the stairs and made sure to kick against the back of each step as he did so. He was getting satisfaction from all that until he heard his father call to him again.

"Git yer ass over here right now, young man!" He bellowed from the living room. Stitch slowly reversed his direction and returned to his father. Stitch was still upset with being the one who had to miss out on the show, so he didn't look Leon in the eye as his father spoke. Instead, he turned and looked at the television, where Cornelius, and Rudolph and the little Dentist Elf were riding an ice berg away from the Bumble. He was so mesmerized by the cartoon that he didn't even realize Leon was talking until a sharp, loud sting consumed the right side of his face and head. Immediately, Stitch let out a yell and started to cry as he noticed his father's large finger pointing in his face, "Look at me when I talk to you, you little shit, or I'll smack the other side of your face!" Stitch continued to cry as Leon scolded him.

"I... I just wanna watch the show." Leon said through sobs and tears.

"Then sit yer ass down and watch the fuckin' show." Leon cursed through clenched teeth. "And if I hear one more peep outta you; you're going straight to bed, do you understand, young man?"

Suddenly, the sting to his face wasn't so bad and Stitch walked back to his little bowl and sat down to watch the rest of the show.

Christmas would come & go, and there would always be the next Holiday Season to watch those cartoons again. Stitch thought about how those shows were on DVD and VHS tapes; and how one could probably even find them posted on some Internet Video hosting site. ***It's just not the same anymore. It's almost like there is no magic left in Christmas*.** Stitch thought to himself as he turned and walked away. He walked down the middle of the one-way street towards the Cohoes Waterfalls. Once there, he stopped at the over look and lit a cigarette drawing in a lungful of smoke. As he exhaled, he recalled how he, Jared and Arnold would hang-out in that very spot and 'bust one another's balls'. As Stitch flicked the ash from his cigarette as he began thinking about his two best friends when he was suddenly struck with sadness as he remembered the day he heard about Arnold dying.

Arnold was sick for quite some time after constant pains in his thumbs and knees. The pains were severe enough for Arnold's mother to take him to the doctor's office. After a series of blood tests it was determined that Arnold had Leukemia. Months of radiation treatment and chemotherapy caused Arnold to bloat up and lose his hair. Kids in the neighborhood referred to Arnold as a freak. All except for Stitch and Jared that is. There was a bond between the three of them that couldn't be broken; not even by something as serious as Leukemia. Arnold's illness only fortified that bond. Stitch and Jared made it a point to visit Arnold every day after school where they would hang out in Arnold's house and to keep him company while his mother worked overtime in the mills. When she returned home, she would cook authentic Korean foods for the boys as a way to thank Stitch and Jared for keeping Arnold company while she worked. Jared lived further away and he couldn't always visit with Arnold; but Stitch, on the other hand, lived just around the corner and would be with Arnold everyday. The boys would always talk about growing up and joining the Navy and getting stationed on an aircraft carrier of the coast of Japan or Korea. Arnold kidded how that wouldn't be a good idea for him because they'd accuse him of being a spy or something. That very summer, Arnold informed Jared and Stitch that he was going to Florida for the summer to spend some time with his biological father. That was the last time the three boys would ever be together. Arnold would not return from Florida. Months into the next school year, Arnold's mother, Kim, informed Stitch and Jared that Arnold had lost his battle to Leukemia and died in his father's home. Stitch and Jared spent the entire weekend, camped out at the lookout near the waterfalls with cigarettes and beer. The teenaged boys cried over the loss of their friend and remembered him with stories about the antics and the trouble the three would get into.

Stitch watched his cigarette fly over the fence as he gazed at the waterfalls and the Mohawk River. As he wiped away a tear from his eye, he recalled some words that were engraved on a wall of his barracks in boot camp. "*It's not the years in your life that count. It's the life in your years. - Abe Lincoln*" Stitch smiled as he looked up to the dark, November clouds and thanked Abe Lincoln for those wise words. "We definitely had plenty of life in our years, didn't we, Arnold?"

CHAPTER SEVEN

The Elks Lodge, along the bank of the Mohawk River, was the meeting place for the reunion. The same place as it was for the 20th reunion; however, this was Stitch's first reunion. He had received the other invitations in the mail, but he could never bring himself to attend. However, he made sure to make it to this one. Stitch smirked and dropped his cigarette to the ground and crushed it out with his well-shined shoes. As he approached the building he noticed cars pulling into the parking lot. Some cars were elegant while others could barely be called cars. Stitch pulled his invitation from the inner breast pocket of his jacket as he approached the main entrance of the building. He was greeted with a smile and a familiar face that looked at him with quandary. She was an attractive woman for her age and her body was in better shape than most girls half her age. However, the crow's feet in the corners of her eyes gave away her age. That and the fact that she was in his graduating class, that is.

"Are you here for the Class of 1982?" she asked as she tried to figure out whom it was that stood before her.

"Yes, Celine." Stitch replied with a coy smile. "You don't remember me?" he asked with a wider, more playful grin. It was no wonder Celine Tyler was unable to recall the face that stared at her own. Stitch was now a large, burly man. Quite the opposite of when he was the skinny, lanky kid that swung on the swing set in her back yard and ate cookies and drank lemonade until the street lights came on. His face was roughened and sported a goatee, as opposed to the baby-faced, hairless mug that he had as a teenager in high school. His head was shaven, giving him an almost sinister look. Rather than the shy, boyish look he had as a young man.

"Of course I do." Celine lied. She glanced down at his invitation and when she noticed his name a surprised look lit up her face. "Stitch LeRue?" she said. Suddenly her eyes widened as she noticed the boy she remembered in the eyes of the man that stood before her. "OH MY GOD!" her face had shown such disbelief. "You look terrific; how are you?"

"I'm doing ok." He said shyly, as if he were that boy that rode his bike to her house in the summertime. He had such a crush on her and he could feel the old, boyish feelings coming back to him as he stood before her. "You look incredible, you haven't changed a bit." He truly meant what he said. She looked just as she did when they were in High School. She was his secret crush, but he would never say so. In all actuality, she was every boy's secret crush.

"You have to sit with us." She said as she handed him a table assignment. "We'll be at table twenty."

"I'll be waiting." Stitch said as he accepted the table assignment and allowed her to pin his 'Hello My Name Is:' tag onto the lapel of his jacket.

Stitch walked into the main lobby area and looked around at all his old classmates. Many faces he did not recognize, while others were faces that were unmistakable. As he scoped the table's centerpieces for numbers, he noticed something peculiar. Everyone was standing in cliques. It was odd, but all these years after school had graduated, these people were still standing in cliques. Those who were cheerleaders were all standing next to the main doors, while the jocks were all standing near the bar. Table five and table twelve, which were set next to each other, held the freaks and geeks of the class of 1982. Stitch looked for table twenty to see who was sitting there. He was sure there would be a circle of 'nobodies' at this table but to his surprise were some of the more popular students. He began to feel very uncomfortable as he approached with his table assignment. Immediately he recognized Dave Galicki. Suddenly, Stitch grew nervous as he feared what Dave might say about his shoes. He felt like that gawky kid from all those years ago. He thought about the way he felt in gym class when Dave made fun of the shoes his mother had purchased for him all those years ago. Stitch had been embarrassed at that time, but now he was more angry than anything else. He knew that *his* parents had done their best for him, under the circumstances, and he was proud that his parents found a way to cut corners in order to survive and make ends meet. It bothered Stitch that Dave didn't know anything about how Stitch's family had lived and that fat, pudgy, little bastard probably wouldn't have lasted a day if *his* parents had to do the things that Stitch's parents did. Stitch puffed out his chest and almost hoped that the fat, balding, pretentious, little dick-headed bastard would just try to embarrass him.

Stitch placed his seating assignment at an empty chair and unbuttoned his jacket's inner button and seated himself. The conversation around the table didn't stop as he sat. It was just like high school all over again. He was invisible to them. Dave stood speaking to a small group while in a pair of khaki slacks with a navy blue sports coat and a light blue shirt and no tie. He was fatter than he was in high school and his comb over hairstyle made Stitch want to laugh. He was the same height as when he was in Middle School. He was short, fat and balding. ***Marge would love this***. He said to himself. He regarded Dave some more and assumed that he was a blue-collar worker, unlike that of Derrick Dodson who stood next to Dave. Derrick looked over the head of Dave as he noticed Stitch looking at him. He squinted his eyes as if it would help him to see better. Derrick was sure that he knew this guy, but he just wasn't sure exactly who it was until Stitch smiled and nodded acknowledgement to him.

"Stitch?" Derrick asked. "Stitch LeRue?"

As Stitch stood up to shake Derrick's hand, the group around the table suddenly became quiet. "Holy shit, man!" Derrick said with a slight laugh. "I hardly recognized you!" He patted Stitch on his shoulder as he shook his hand. "I guess the Navy was good for you, huh?"

It pleased Stitch that Derrick remembered him joining the Navy. "You look like your doing well." Stitch joked as he flipped a finger across the lapel of Derrick's Armani suit jacket. "What kind of work do you do?"

"I don't." Derrick replied with a smile. "I started a Dot Com company back in the early nineties and it's been all good from there."

"Internet Day Trading?" Stitch guessed.

"No, no." Derrick said as he shook his head. "I have a distribution company and all my orders are filled by…" Derrick stopped and waved away the rest of the conversation. "You know what." He said more as a statement than a question. "It's too boring to get into; let's just say I'm doing well and leave it at that."

Derrick turned to the rest of the crowd and introduced Stitch. Most of them he knew and others were spouses of his old classmates. Stitch was pleased to see that most of the people from school were more human as adults than they were as kids. Derrick continued introducing everyone as if he was the host of the event.

"And this is Tom Davies." Derrick said as he introduced Stitch to a tall man with dark hair. He had a bit of silver whisked into his sideburns and along his temples. More of a salt-n-pepper look than anything else but it suited him.

As Stitch shook the man's hand, Derrick explained that Tom was Celine Tyler's husband. On the outside, Stitch gave a small 'pleasantly surprised' look with his eyes. However, on the inside he was completely jealous and hoped that it wasn't showing. Fortunately, Tom Davies didn't see the bit of green in Stitch's blue eyes.

"It's a pleasure to meet you." Stitch said, shaking the man's hand. "Are you from this area?" Stitch hated meeting new people. He never knew what to say or how he'd sound as he said it.

"I'm from Farmingdale." Tom replied. "Long Island." He replied quickly as not to be rude, but then immediately asked a question, which happened to be the one question that Stitch hadn't ever gotten used to in his entire adulthood.

"Is your name really Stitch?" the man asked. "Or is that just a nick-name?"

Stitch hated that question and he especially hated when people asked him about that little blue alien cartoon character. However, over the years Stitch learned to shake it off, smile and tell the story of how he got his name.

It was the 60's and my parents were kinda like flower children or beatniks or whatever they were called in those days. My father was twenty-five years old and my mother was seventeen. The two used to spend their time sucking on sugar cubes coated with LSD and talking about how they would change the world. You know, typical liberal thinking. Anyhow, the two married and soon my mother became pregnant. When the time came, she went into labor and remained in labor for 117 hours. Nearly a week she dealt with labor pains and contractions. I know this, because my entire life, whenever I hurt her feelings she would tell me, "I suffered 117 hours of pain for you and this is the way you treat me!" *So trust me as I tell you these facts. It turned out that I was a breech baby. I came out backwards. Except I didn't come out headfirst, no sir; I came out ass first! My ankles were up around my head and I came into the world showing my backside. However, my mother was a little woman at the time and her pelvis couldn't take the strain so the doctor's had to cut into my mother to get me out. Once I was free and clear, they had to "STITCH" her back up. She and my father named me "STITCH" as a way of letting me know my mother's pain, as they put it. My birth certificate reads: STITCH NMN LeRUE. But My grandmother wouldn't have it and she refused to call me "Stitch" and referred to me only as* "The Boy". *Whenever she wanted to know about me she would ask,* "How's The Boy today?" *or she'd say,* "Can I take The Boy to the city with me?" *But when I was three-years-old, my parents finally sobered up and stopped dropping acid and they named me after my father. However, since I'd been called "Stitch" for so many years, it just stayed as such. Now, the only people who refer to me as Leon LeRue are bill collectors and lawyers. So I just kept it "Stitch".*

Tom Davies was in awe of this story. He smiled the entire time it was being told and believed every word of it. The truth was, Stitch's parents were not hippies, nor did they do drugs. Stitch's mother really was in labor for 117 hours and Stitch really was born breech and ass first. But to tell people that he was called Stitch because of an injury to his head as a baby was just too boring a story. Stitch liked to embellish the story a little bit.

"What did the *NMN* stand for on your birth certificate?" Derrick asked.

"It means *No Middle Name.*" Stitch replied without missing a beat. He had told this story thousands of times and had actually seen NMN on a buddies ID card during boot camp. He thought it was too cool and adapted it for his story.

"Wow!" Dave Galicki said. "I never knew that about you." Dave took a sip of his beer and walked over and extended his hand to Stitch. "How the hell have ya' been?" Dave asked waiting for Stitch to take his hand.

Stitch grabbed Dave's hand and gave a firm, solid handshake, but noticed Dave's grip was loose and his hand was moist. ***A sign of weakness.*** Stitch thought to himself. "I'm doing well, Dave." Stitch replied while looking the man directly in the eye. "How have things been for you?"

"Oh, doing pretty good." Dave replied. However, he averted his eyes to the left and down. ***Sign of deceit***. Stitch thought. ***He hasn't changed a bit.***

After talking with Dave, Stitch moved on and spoke with Tom Davies for few moments before Derrick called Stitch over to the bar for a drink. Stitch shook Tom's hand and told him he was glad to have met him. "We'll talk again soon." Tom said as Derrick led Stitch away. Stitch normally disliked meeting new people, but he genuinely enjoyed talking with Tom and getting to know him. He was starting to think that he hadn't made a mistake by attending after all.

"What are you drinking?" Derrick asked.

"Gentleman Jack, neat." Stitch replied. He had grown a taste for the whiskey.

Derrick ordered two drinks from the bartender and pulled out a hundred dollar bill to pay for them. "Let me get this first round, ok?" Derrick asked.

"No complaints from this end." Stitch replied with a smile.

Stitch looked around the room and started to notice more faces, but found it difficult to put names to them. As he stood at the bar next to Derrick, someone tapped on Stitch's shoulder. He simply turned around and looked at the familiar face.

"STITCH!" The man said with a wide grin. "How the hell are ya'!"

Stitch was at a loss for the man's name. He knew the face and kept his eyes there. He refrained from glancing down at the man's nametag as he improvised. "HEY..." ***what the hell is his name? What the hell is his name!*** "...MAN!" ***that worked – I'll keep using 'man'!*** "I'm good, how have you been?"

"Things are great!" The man replied. As he spoke, Derrick turned around with Stitch's drink and the man's attention went to Derrick, allowing Stitch to look at his nametag. ***Todd Logan!*** He thought to himself. ***Of course!***

This kind of thing happened all night long for Stitch. He found it more and more difficult to remember the names of familiar faces. Not all of them, just the ones who he didn't really interact with during school. He remembered the pretty girls who didn't talk to him and he recalled the names of the guys who gave him a hard time.

But the others...

Those who didn't see him or made him feel as though he were invisible; he had no idea who they were. He found this to be ironic that as a kid he was invisible to them and now they were a mystery to him.

Stitch sat at his table and wondered if Jared would show up. The two of them were thick as thieves in school and to be here without him was almost blasphemous. Suddenly, Stitch heard his name mentioned in the conversation that going on at his table.

"... You remember that don't you, Stitch?" Celine said from across the table. But Stitch hadn't been paying attention and a look of curiosity covered his face.

"Aw, c'mon man." Derrick said. "How could you have forgotten Mr. Weiment's class?

Suddenly, Stitch remembered his old home-room teacher from middle school. "What about him?" Stitch asked as he sat up close to the table and got in on the conversation.

"Don't you remember that day that you were goofing off and Weiment came up and grabbed your ear?" Derrick suddenly struck a memory that Stitch had thought he'd buried away forever. He'd remembered it earlier, but he'd forgotten bits and pieces of that story.

SEPTEMBER 1976

Stitch sat in the back of the classroom with Derrick Dodson. The two would sit in the back and talk about the radio disk jockey they heard that morning on WTRY. Stitch would imitate the DJ as he recalled some of the skits from the show. Derrick would always laugh and tell Stitch he should be a DJ. Meanwhile, Mr. Weiment was calling attendance.

"LeRue." Mr. Weiment said without looking up from his roll call roster. However, Stitch had his back turned to the front of the room as he was still chattering with Derrick. "Mr. LeRue?" The teacher said louder, with a touch of annoyance. However, Stitch was still goofing off with Derrick and his eyes were closed so he couldn't see the look on Derrick's face that would have warned him that Mr. Weiment had walked up and was standing right behind him. The teacher leaned in close to Stitch and nearly yelled, "MISTER LeRUE!"

Stitch literally jumped out of his chair as he spun around and looked up at his teacher with surprise.

"Do I have your attention now, Mr. LeRue?" He said sarcastically.

"Yes." Stitch replied with annoyance. He was infuriated on the inside, but tried not to let it show. He was grinding his teeth and anger burned in his belly. "Jerk." Stitch whispered under his breath as Weiment started to walk away. However, Stitch realized his comment was a tad too loud when Mr. Weiment stopped in his tracks and a couple girls gasped with surprise at Stitch. Stitch's eyes darted around the room, looking for something else that might have caught Mr. Weiment's attention or made the girls gasp. But Mr. Weiment turned and looked directly at Stitch.

"WHAT DID YOU SAY TO ME?" The teacher bellowed. His accent thickened with anger.

Stitch knew that there was no turning back from this and he tried to sit up in his seat and look innocent. He didn't deny anything, but he knew better than to repeat what he said. Therefore, he just sat there and said nothing as he locked his gaze on Weiment's. The teacher walked up to Stitch and stood alongside his desk in an imposing manner and yelled at him.

"GET UP!" He yelled.

Stitch sat steadfast. On the outside he looked like he was being rebellious, but on the inside he was too scared to do anything. He had never heard Mr. Weiment yell like that before and he had no idea what to do.

"I SAID GET UP!" The teacher reached out and grabbed Stitch by his ear and yanked him out of his chair. A searing pain shot through Stitch's ear with a dull 'pop' sound. Stitch reached for the teacher's hand and tried to pull it away, but his grip was too firm and all Stitch could do was grab at the teacher's wrist when he suddenly had a 'mom moment' and blurted out an angry obscenity.

"LET GO OF ME YOU ASSHOLE!" Stitch yelled. He knew he would get into more trouble, but the pain was so intense that he couldn't help himself. He hoped that the obscenity would shock the teacher enough to let go. Instead it only caused him to tug harder.

"JESUS CHRIST!" Stitch yelled out. "THAT FUCKIN' HURTS!!" Stitch was near tears as the class gasped at Stitch's outbursts. Suddenly there were laughs and cheers.

"YOU TELL 'EM, STITCH!" someone called out from the right side of the room.

As the teacher pulled him closer to the door, Stitch let out one last blast to get his classmate's attention.

"LET ME GO YOU FUCKIN' JERK-OFF!" Stitch yelled as Weiment pulled him into the hallway. Stitch heard an uproar of laughter coming from the classroom and suddenly felt like he was a big man on campus.

"Oh my god." Celine said as she laughed at the memory. "I nearly peed my pants that day."

"What did Weiment do?" Derrick asked. "You never did tell us what happened."

Stitch sat in awe. When that incident happened, he went from being the funny-guy right back to being the "nobody". He didn't think anyone cared about what happened to him. Apparently, he was the talk of the morning and didn't even know it. When he left the principle's office, it was as if it never happened. No one came up to talk to him; nor did anyone pat him on the shoulder for making them laugh. His day just went back to being the same crappy day that it had always been.

"I didn't wanna bring it up, man." Dave said. "You looked pissed when you came out of the Principle's office. But that's why I picked you for relay races that day, you showed some balls!"

It all made sense to Stitch now. He remembered the relay races and the K-Mart shoes that he had to wear that day. Dave picked him for his team because he stood up to Mr. Weiment and showed them that he wasn't a geek or a puss or whatever they called him behind his back. At least not until he fell on his face and lost the relay race for his team. Then he reverted back to being the 'nobody' that he was.

Mr. Weiment walked Stitch to the Principle's office door. "Now you go in there and tell Mr. Archibald what you said!" He opened the door for Stitch and then heard his classroom getting louder. "I'll be back in a moment."

The class must have been causing quite the commotion, because Mr. Weiment never showed back up at the Principle's office.

Stitch sat and waited to be called in to see the principle, Mr. Archibald. The large, oak door slowly opened behind the secretary's desk and a very large, bearded man appeared from behind the door. "Mr. LeRue, could you come in here please?" The Principle said calmly.

Stitch got up from his chair and walked past the secretary with baby steps and wiped his sweaty palms on his jeans. "You wanted to see me, Sir?" Stitch's eyes widened when he looked up and noticed his sister standing in the room. He was confused and didn't understand what happened between leaving homeroom and showing up at the principles office. It was less than twenty seconds walk, *how did she get called into this*?.

"Caitlin?" he said, wondering why she was looking so afraid. Her eyes were red, as if she'd been crying. "What are you doing here?"

"Your sister has been telling her teachers and classmates some very interesting stories." Mr. Archibald said.

The principle walked around his desk and then sat in his large chair. "Apparently, your father is a blind-drunk who has to be helped out of the gutter on a daily basis." The principle said as he eyed Stitch's sister. "According to your sister, your father can not stay sober and takes too much medication and drinks all your family's money." Stitch couldn't believe what he was hearing. Caitlin must have been telling stories to gain attention and now it was about to backfire on her. "Is this true, Mr. LeRue?"

Stitch looked at his sister's pleading eyes and then looked back to his principle, who sat in an assuming manner at his large, cluttered desk. Stitch wanted to protect his sister and stick up for her, but not at the expense of his father. "No, Sir." Stitch replied, looking away from his sister's eyes. He could hear her sob and weep.

"Go back to your classroom, young lady." Mr. Archibald instructed. "I want a moment alone with your brother."

As Caitlin slowly closed the door, she kept her eyes on her brother. They were sad, betrayed eyes that slowly disappeared behind the closing door.

"I will not embarrass your parents by calling this to them." The Principle said. "I will, however, ask that you tell your parents what transpired here, today."

Stitch sat dumbfounded. He was waiting for the roof to cave in on him. Any moment, Weiment would walk through the door. "Yes, Sir." Was all Stitch could say.

"I know you may want to stick up for your sister and protect her." He said. "But for your parents' sake, you need to tell them what she has been saying."

Was that the door opening? Stitch wondered as he turned around quickly but to his pleasant surprise, the door was still shut. He turned back to his principle and assured him that he will pass it along to his parents.

"Very well." Mr. Archibald replied.

Stitch sat still and waited for the ball to drop. He just knew that it was his turn to get yelled at.

"Is there something else, Mr. LeRue?" The Principle asked.

Stitch thought for a moment and decided to keep his throbbing ear to himself. "No, Sir." He said quickly.

"Then get back to your class."

Stitch jumped up out of the chair and ran from the principle's office and past the secretary's desk. It was then that he realized that the classroom's loud noises were more than a distraction and pulled Weiment back, thus keeping him from saying anything to the Principle. Stitch was feeling better about his day so far. Just as he reached the hallway, he heard the bell ring, signaling that homeroom was over. Stitch ran to his locker to grab his books but was confronted by his sister. She was still crying and she pleaded with him not to tell their father.

"Please don't tell dad, Stitch. Please!" The look on her face was pathetic. Tears ran down her cheeks as she bargained with her brother. "I'll never do it again, I promise! Just DON'T TELL THEM!"

"I have to, Caitlin." Stitch replied softly. "I'm sorry, but Mr. Archibald told me that I have to." Stitch closed his locker and walked away, leaving his sister standing there alone. He didn't need to turn around to see the fear and sadness in her eyes. He could feel it emanating from her.

"So c'mon, man." Dave said. "What happened with Archibald?"

"Nothing." Stitch lied. Weiment never came back and then the bell rang, so I got the hell out of there."

"WHOA!" Exclaimed Todd Logan. "Talk about being lucky!"

Stitch smirked at the remark. *If only they knew.* He thought to himself. They wouldn't think I was so lucky having to find out what I did.

Stitch told his parents what had happened at school and Caitlin got a beating like Stitch had never seen or heard in all his life. Part of him felt guilty for her. She was getting a beating for talking about their father, yet Stitch escaped punishment for cursing at his teacher and causing a disruption in the classroom. He genuinely felt for his sister, but was partly glad that he'd been able to escape such a punishment. However, he knew he'd be back in some type of trouble and would be getting punished eventually. It was inevitable.

CHAPTER EIGHT

Stitch sat at the table with his back facing the back-wall bar. His gaze was locked past Celine and Brenda who were reminiscing old times. Stitch had been sitting amongst these people who were just mere reflections of the kids he had once known. Celine was the beautiful, young girl for whom he had a secret crush. Brenda was one of the cheerleader types, who hung around with the jocks and made life hell for all the norms and dorks in the class.

As Stitch sat and stared toward the main entrance, two soft, warm hands suddenly blocked his vision and a soft voice whispered in his ear, "Remember me?"

Stitch thought for a moment and tried to place a face to the voice, however, the bouquet of her perfume was distracting him. She smelled elegant, but he knew that all the females in his class would have nothing to do with him. *Who could this be?* He thought to himself.

Slowly the hands slide away from his eyes and Stitch turned to find an attractive woman. She was thin and her hair was brown with tiny streaks of silver. Stitch stared at her face for what seemed like an eternity but could not recall a name for this woman.

"It's me!" she said with excitement. "*Courtney*!"

Stitch still looked mystified. *Courtney?* He thought to himself. ***The only Courtney I ever knew was short and very heavy...*** He let his thought trail off and took a stab at her name. "Courtney Grabowski?" he asked with a quizzical look.

"YEAH!" She said, surprised that he was able to remember her name. "Well, it's Kramer now." She said, showing her wedding and engagement rings on her left hand. "I've been married for seventeen years now."

Stitch stood up and offered to shake her hand but Courtney wouldn't hear of it. She insisted that he hug her. Everyone at the table was looking at the two of them and Stitch shrugged his shoulders with his eyes, letting them know that he was just as confused as they were.

"Everyone." He said, trying to get the table's attention. "You all remember Courtney

Grabowski, don't you?" Stitch was sure they would all look at one another and wonder who the hell he was talking about. Courtney wasn't one of the popular girls and he was sure they would do or say something to hurt her feelings as they did all those years ago. But to Stitch's surprise, everyone stood up and hugged Courtney in the fashion that old friends would do. He couldn't believe what he was seeing. As kids, she was only two or three rungs up on the social ladder from Large Marge, and now here they were acting like they were old friends who shared recipes and traded coupons during bridge night. Stitch stepped back from the crowd walked towards the front entrance of the building. A part of him wanted to leave and get away from these people, but something else was making him stay. He told himself that what kids did back then were the actions of children who may or may not have known better. Either way, they were still children. The people in the room with him at that moment were no longer children; they were adults who may or may not have known better. Stitch was glad to know that he could feel more comfortable amongst these people now, regardless of the past. ***It's just too bad I couldn't get Marge to come with me.*** He thought to himself.

Stitch reached into his breast pocket and pulled out a pack of cigarettes and headed for the smoking area when suddenly a pair of soft, warm hands covered his eyes again. He was all ready to tell Courtney that he knew it was her when he suddenly heard a different female voice in his ear.

Why couldn't I have been this popular when I was actually IN *school?* Stitch thought to himself. *I probably would have had more fun!*

"I've gotta say, Stitch; the bald look suits you. You look hot.." The sexy, husky voice said.

Stitch didn't wait for the hands to pull away. Instead he spun around to find Barbara Marshall standing before him. Stitch froze for a moment and then smiled as Barbara wasn't just another girl from school; she was like family. Stitch's cousin, Vince, had dated Barbara in high school and they were quite an item for some time. To Stitch, she was like a celebrity because in school she was on the cheerleading squad and hung out with the jocks and the popular crowd. But on the weekends, or holidays, she was actually part of Stitch's family when she would show up for the picnics and parties at Stitch's house. She would never 'really' acknowledge him in school, but Stitch understood the order of things. She had a reputation to uphold and to be seen consorting with the lower level echelon of the schools social system would not have been good for her. At least that's how Stitch understood things.

Stitch smiled as he recognized her immediately. Twenty-five years to Barbara was like twenty-five minutes to every other human on this planet. She looked the same as she did in High School and Stitch's heart nearly skipped a beat when she smiled at him.

"I thought you were living in California?" She said as she took his arm and walked out to the main entrance with him.

"Actually, I'm living in Pittsburgh." Stitch replied. He was about to put his cigarettes back in his pocket when Barbara placed her hand on his and asked if she could get a smoke from him. Surprised, Stitch just stared.

"What?" She asked.

"I didn't know you were a smoker." Stitch said as he tapped out a cigarette for her.

"Not in school." She said as she put it to her lips. Stitch clicked open his Zippo and flicked a flame for her. She placed her hand against his and guarded the flame from the wind of the November night. She drew in a breath and the end of her cigarette glowed bright orange. Stitch stared at her with amazement. She actually looked the same exact way she did twenty-five years ago. As she exhaled, she explained, "But when I got to college I started smoking and I've been a smoker ever since."

Stitch lit a cigarette for himself and the two talked about the things that have happened to them over the past twenty-five years. She told Stitch that she was married three times and had two kids who were grown. Stitch felt so old hearing that one of his classmates had kids that were getting ready for college.

"So how about you?" She asked with a smile. "What's been happening with you? Are you still in the Navy?"

Stitch smiled to cover his uncomfortable feels about the subject. "No." He replied plainly. "I've been out for a few years now."

"Retired?" She asked.

Stitch felt like she was poking his brain with a red-hot poker. "Actually, I was medically discharged after 15 years." He drew in on his cigarette. "I've been out for almost ten years, now." He said. He looked away from her and towards the river. He loved the Navy and the life that he had there. The day the medical board told him that he could no longer serve was the worst day of his life. Talking about it over and over was not so therapeutic for him.

Barbara must have heard the sadness in his voice and she placed a hand on his shoulder. "I'm sorry." She said with a gentle squeeze. "I didn't mean to pry."

Stitch smiled at her, hoping to ease the tension that was suddenly surrounding them. "It's okay." He said with a wink. "Really. Things are good for me."

Barbara's eyes seemed to sparkle as she looked into Stitch's eyes. A small smile crept up on her face and she took his hand. Stitch had no idea what she was thinking or what she was doing as she guided him back into the hall. Twenty-five years ago he would have killed for this opportunity. ***Hell!*** He thought. ***Every guy in our school would have killed for this opportunity!***

Barbara stopped in the middle of the empty dance floor.

"Would you care to dance, sir?" She said playfully.

"It would be my pleasure, m'lady." He replied with a small smile.

Stitch could hardly believe what was happening. He was dancing cheek to cheek with Barbara Marshall and no one was pointing a gun at her temple. *She* asked *him* to dance with *her*!

"You look really good." She said as she stood back from him and smiled. "It's been real nice seeing you again."

Stitch knew the dance was over but he didn't want to let go. When the lights came up and the song ended, she leaned in and gave Stitch a small peck on the cheek.

"It was really good seeing you again." She said once more. "Thanks for the cigarette."

"Anytime." Stitch replied with a silly look on his face. "Anytime, indeed." He said more quietly to himself as she walked away. All those years in school when he was laughed at by the girls and was the subject of ridicule and giggles; all those times were suddenly erased with just three minutes of dancing with Barbara Marshall the Home Coming Queen. The Prom Queen. The Most Popular Girl in the school. Stitch knew she had no idea how much that had meant to him. He wondered if she would ever realized how much faith she restored in his idea of women. Some say that time heals all pain, but Stitch knew that Time *and Barbara Marshall* heal pain a hell of a lot quicker!

"Was that Barbara Marshall?" A familiar voice from behind Stitch said.

"Yeah." Stitch replied absently as he watched her walk away.

"Who'd have ever thought that *you*, of all people, would ever get a dance with Barbara Marshall, let alone get a kiss from her."

Before Stitch could get too angry, he spun around to see who could be stupid enough to try and embarrass him. He unclenched his fist just as he noticed his best friend, Jared standing there with a silly smirk on his face. Part of Stitch wanted to cry and another part of him wanted to scream out with joy, but instead, he maintained his composure and simply offered his longtime friend a hug.

Jared threw his arms wide and the two men embraced in a hug that anyone could see was brotherly. If there was anyone on this planet that could make Stitch feel young again, it was Jared.

"HOLY SHIT, DUDE!" Stitch said, as he stepped back from Jared and took a look at him. "How the hell are you?"

"You would know the answer to that question if you would call or write once in a while." Jared responded sarcastically while flicking his middle finger at Stitch's nose. "How's your mom doing?"

"She's good." Stitch replied. He was glad that the first person Jared asked about was Stitch's mother. There were so many times that Jared would get pissed off with his own parents that he would go to Stitch's house to stay with them. He was there so much that he started calling Gerti, 'Mom'. She liked him and she liked the fact that he felt safe at their house.

Friday, June 16th 1978

The school year was coming to a close. There were only three more school days left and then the summer would begin. Stitch was excited to be getting out of school and was looking forward to spending his summer catching frogs, or climbing the waterfalls or swimming in the "king's chair" on the top of the falls.

Caitlin came into the living room with their cousin, Danielle and plopped on the couch.

"We're gonna watch the wacky races." she said as she walked over to the television console.

"I don't care." Stitch spat back. He wanted to be alone, but he knew that wasn't ever going to happen in the LeRue house. Earl was up in their room, playing with army men and his dad was in the kitchen cooking dinner, regardless of the fact that it was only 3:30 in the afternoon. The living room was the last place where Stitch could hang out alone, but now even that was gone.

As Caitlin pulled out the little knob, to turn on the TV, she stomped her foot in anger.

"HEY!" She yelled. She pushed the knob in and then pulled it out more forcefully this time. When the television didn't turn on, she got real angry. "DAD!" She screamed at the top of her lungs.

"KNOCK IT OFF IN THERE!" Leon yelled back from the kitchen.

"DAD. THE TELEVISION WON'T TURN ON!" Caitlin yelled again. Stitch shook his head in disbelief as he walked out of the living room. *Why does everyone have to yell in this house?* He thought as he exited through the kitchen and down the stairs to the front stoop where he was free of all the yelling and could just sit and relax.

"What the hell is your sister yelling about?" Gerti asked, nearly scaring Stitch to death. He didn't see her sitting in lawn chair at the base of the front stoop. She had a glass of Pepsi and a copy of the TV GUIDE on her lap. She was doing the crossword puzzle and stopped when Stitch let the big, green door slam behind him.

"She's mad because the TV won't turn on." Stitch replied.

"That's gonna be hard to do with no electricity." Gerti replied nonchalantly. She picked up the TV GUIDE and started doing the crossword puzzle again.

Stitch sat quietly, trying to figure out why there would be no electricity and deduced that his parents weren't able to pay the bill and were shut off again.

"How long before it gets turned back on?" Stitch asked, trying to make conversation with his mother.

"I don't know." Gerti replied without looking up from her magazine. "I guess in three or four months, depending on the weather." She said casually; as if she were talking about a book she read; like it was no big deal.

Stitch was baffled. He stared at her in amazement and wondered why it would take so long to get the electricity turned back on or what role the weather played in that determination.

"Wow." He said plainly. "How big of bill do we owe?"

"*WE*" his mother repeated with sarcasm. "Since when do *WE* pay the bills?" She asked, implying that there is no '*WE*' to the discussion.

"WE don't owe anything." She replied. "I had them shut it off for the summer so 'I' can save some money."

Stitch couldn't believe what he was hearing. His mother actually had the electricity turned off. *No television, no radio... what are we going to do?* He thought to himself. And just when he thought things couldn't get any worse, she poured a little salt in his wounds...

"I had the phone turned off too." Again, she said it as easily as if she were talking about how easy it was to flush the toilet. Stitch couldn't believe what he was hearing. He was a teen-aged boy and the television and phone were a necessity for a teenager, He sat on the stoop and stared slack-jawed at his mother. He started thinking how karma had come up to bite him in the ass. Caitlin got her ass beat for telling bad stories about their father and Stitch got away with swearing at his teacher in class. This was the payback.

"But what about..."

"Lights?" She finished for him. "It's summertime. The sun doesn't set until after nine o'clock."

"Yeah, but what about..."

"Television?" She finished again, almost anticipating his questions. "It's summertime and it's all re-runs. You've seen those shows aready. Go out and play with you friends."

"Yeah, but how about..."

"The phone?"

Damned! She's too friggin' good at this!

"Go to their house and talk to them. You don't need the phone."

Stitch could hear Caitlin carrying on, upstairs, inside the house. She was stomping her feet and crying about not being able to watch the 'Wacky Races'. In some sick, twisted way, this made the situation tolerable for Stitch just knowing that Caitlin hated it so much.

Stitch leaned his head back against the rough brick wall and closed his eyes. He listened to the sounds of the pigeons in the alley. He could hear the 'ping' of a basketball being bounce and realized it was Stosh coming back from the basketball court. He heard the sounds of running feet coming down the street, from the direction of the waterfalls. Stitch stared at the clouds and blue sky as he absorbed the sounds and then realized that the running feet had stopped in front of his stoop and was accompanied by heavy breathing. Stitch looked down and seen Jared bent over and gasping for air. Gerti got up from her seat and approached the boy.

"Jared?" She said. "What's wrong? Are you all right?"

"I'm fine." Jared said as he caught his breath. "Just running too much."

Stitch could see that something was wrong. He had known Jared since the second grade and knew when something was wrong with him. It had to be bad if he didn't want to tell Gerti about it.

"You wanna go to the park?" Stitch asked, trying to rescue his friend from his mother's prying.

"Nah." Jared replied, obviously not understanding what was Stitch was trying to do.

"You wanna go up to my room and hang out?" Stitch asked. As Jared looked up, Stitch shot his eyes in the direction of his mother, letting Jared know that he wanted to get away so the two of them could talk.

Jared must have understood. "Uhm... Yeah, sure." He replied quickly.

"Oh wait." Stitch said as he realized there was no electricity to power their radio. "Let's just go to the park."

The two boys walked across Mohawk Street and to Craner Park, where Jared told Stitch about a fight he had had with his father.

"He's so friggin' unreasonable!" Jared said, trying to hold back his tears. "I hate that son-of-a-bitch!" But he could hold them back no longer. Jared started to cry.

Jared's father was a Fireman and his mother was worked in a bank. The two of them made a nice living, which enabled them to live up on the hill. Jared lived in a modest ranch style house with an in-ground pool and a garage and he had a really cool room in the basement that his father had built for him. From what Stitch could tell, there was never a lack of money in Jared's family, at least not like what Stitch was used to seeing. Jared always had the cool new shoes and the popular clothes. But there was something about Jared that kept him from being good friends with the Jocks and the Prissies and all the other people who made life hell for them. Jared and Stitch were two of a kind. If you didn't know better, you would swear the two were brothers.

Jared's father was a large, burly man and from what Stitch knew of him, he was very strict. There were times that Jared and his father would get into physical fights and his dad would literally throw him out of the house. This was one of those times. Jared didn't clean up the backyard like he was told to do and his father went ballistic on him. He grabbed Jared by the neck and led him to the backyard to show him what he had forgotten, but Jared was sick of his father's hands grabbing at him and smacking him. This time he fought back. Jared spun out from his father's grasp and smacked his arm to the side as he sidestepped out of father's reach. He told Stitch how his father grabbed him by his hair and yelled in his face. But Jared pushed off and ran from his father. He ran all the way down Manor Avenue to Mohawk Street and all the way down Mohawk Street to School Street without stopping. He told Stitch that he kept running until he found himself on Cataract Street and in front of Stitch's house.

"I'm never going back there!" Jared exclaimed. "I friggin' HATE that bastard!"

"Where are you gonna go?" Stitch asked, worried that he'd never see his friend again.

"I don't know." Jared replied. "I didn't think that far ahead yet." When he looked up, Stitch could see something in Jared's eyes. Something that told Stitch that Jared wasn't bluffing about this. He didn't want to see his friend leave, nor did he want to see him in trouble. He couldn't imagine Jared living on the streets, or sleeping behind a garbage dumpster or eating out of the trash. They had already lost Arnold, there was no way they were going to lose one another.

"You wanna stay with us?" Stitch said.

"Would your parents let me?" Jared said as he perked up at the idea.

"C'mon, man." Stitch said as he put an elbow in Jared's ribs. "My mom friggin' loves you." He said with a smile.

"But you'd have to get used to drinking powdered milk." Stitch joked.

"Mmm. My favorite." Jared joked back.

"And you'd have live without electricity and a phone for the entire summer." Stitch said, trying to ease the chance of embarrassment.

"It'll be like camping!" Jared said as he reached up and tried to flick Stitch's nose, but Stitch was able to deflect it.

Stitch laughed to himself when he realized that Jared was right. Jared had a way of seeing the brighter side of things, as long as it didn't pertain to his parents or his home life.

The two boys walked back to Stitch's house and kicked a plastic bottle along the way.

"Did you eat yet?" Stitch asked as he kicked the bottle out in front of them.

"Not yet." Jared replied. When he reached the bottle, he gave it a good kick that sent it spinning nearly fifteen feet ahead of them.

"My dad is making spaghetti if you want to eat with us." Stitch said smiling. Jared turned and looked at Stitch in horror as he recalled the last time Leon made spaghetti. All the spaghetti noodles were stuck together in a large, column of pre-al Dante pasta noodles. They looked cooked on the outside, but were quite raw and crunchy on the inside.

"Are you kidding with me?" Jared asked in a serious tone.

"Nah." Stitch replied with a small laugh. "I'm just bustin' Yer balls." Stitch reached over and flicked Jared on tip of his nose with his middle finger.

Back at his house, Stitch told his mother what was happening with Jared and his dad, and asked if Jared could stay with them.

"Jared's dad was already here looking for him." Gerti replied. "I told him that the two of you went to the park."

"We must have just missed him." Jared said with relief.

It was starting to get dark and the house was being cast in shadows as Jared and Stitch sat on the sofa and talked about going to the Roller Skating Rink. One of Jared's friends worked there as a roller guard and had told Jared how so many girls hung out there. Stitch knew he had to go there since these would be girls that didn't know him from school. They wouldn't know him as the "DORK" or the "GEEK" or whatever name he was referred as. These would be girls from other schools with no influences. As the two boys talked about how awesome it would be to go to such a place, the front door opened up and Gerti walked in. She nodded her head in the direction of the door as she told Jared that '*someone*' was there to see him. Stitch got nervous as Jared's father walked into the living room and Jared shot up to his feet. He looked like a trapped rat and Stitch wasn't sure what was going to happen.

"I'm not going home." Jared said. He made it a statement, but Stitch could hear the nervousness in his friend's voice.

"I'm not asking you to come home." His father replied.

"I'm serious!" Jared yelled. "Tell Mom that I'm staying here."

Apparently Jared didn't hear his father correctly and Stitch kicked his foot in Jared's direction.

"I said you don't have to come home." Jared's father reiterated. He reached back and grabbed a garbage bag and tossed it into the middle of the living room floor. "You mother thought you might need your clothes."

What the hell is it with Parents and Garbage bags as luggage? Stitch thought to his self as the image of the garbage bag brought forth a horrifying memory.

Jared stared at the garbage bag. He couldn't believe that his parents were going along with this. Stitch stared at the garbage bag as well; but for different reasons. Stitch shuddered inwardly.

"I'm serious." Jared said, snapping Stitch out of his nightmarish daydream.

"We know you're serious." His father said. "That's why we brought you some clothes."Stitch wasn't sure if Jared's dad was being smart or if he just genuinely didn't care. Either way, Jared was able to stay at his place. Every one thought they were brothers; anyway, now they could act as though they were brothers!

Jared bent over and picked up the bag and inspected its contents. When he was satisfied that it had all he would need, he let it fall back to the floor. Jared's father nodded and turned to the door and then stopped. He spoke over his shoulder, without turning around to look at Jared.

"Your mother wants to know if she can attend your graduation ceremony." He said.

Jared looked at Stitch and then to Gerti, who nodded to him, encouraging him to say 'yes'. It was only middle school, but it was a big deal to them.

"Yes." Jared said plainly. He did not look up from the carpet to see his father nod acknowledgment. Only when he heard his father's footsteps descend the front hall stairs did he look up from the floor.

By this time it was getting pretty dark and Gerti started lighting candles on the living room coffee table. Outside the front door, the adults were starting to gather on Leon's front stoop. Art Mitchell, Uncle Dan & Aunt Terri and a few of the other neighbors were already outside the house talking and laughing.

"HEY LEON!" Called out a voice that Stitch hadn't heard in a while. "Git yer ASS down here and have a beer with your brother!"

Stitch ran to the window and seen his Uncle Kyle holding a can of Genesee in one hand and a lit Lucky Strike cigarette in the other.

"DAD!" Stitch called out as he ran into the kitchen. "Uncle Kyle is here!"

Stitch liked when his Uncle Kyle showed up because he would always tell stories of the days when he and Leon were kids. Stitch would hear about fights that his father had been in or antics and trouble they had gotten into. Stitch would always try to imagine his father as a little kid and often wondered what he had looked like. It was fun for him to hear the stories. But if Uncle Kyle stayed too long, He and Leon would get too drunk and then Leon would start crying and slobbering about how messed up his life was.

"Maybe I should go home." Jared said, out of the blue.

"No..." Stitch said. "It'll be fine." He thought Jared might have felt out of place with all the LeRue family congregating on the front porch. "Don't go, it's fun!" Stitch said as he led Jared to the front door by his arm. Jared hesitated and then pulled his arm free.

"I mean, maybe this is bothering my mother and perhaps I should just go home so she won't be sad." Jared said as he kicked at his bag of clothes. Stitch could only imagine what was going through his friend's head. He felt bad for him and wanted him to be happy.

"Just hang out for the night." Stitch said with a smile. "We can call your father in the morning."

Jared smiled and then laughed.

"What's so funny?" Stitch asked. He thought he was being sincere to his friend.

"How loud can you yell?" Jared said, still laughing. "Mom had the phone turned off, remember!"

Stitch wasn't embarrassed by the fact that there was no power. He wasn't ashamed by the fact that his parents had to save money by cutting off the utilities. Without realizing it, Jared had shown him how to laugh at these things. This is what made the two of them so close. The fact that Jared was raised in a home with money; and material things that most kids would kill to have; and yet he didn't judge Stitch or his family for their lack of things. He was a true friend, and Stitch loved him like a brother.

"I'll be sure to tell mom that you asked about her." Stitch said as he led Jared to an open spot at the bar. "Now c'mon and have a drink with me!" Stitch exclaimed. "We have a lot to catch up on!"

CHAPTER NINE

The two men leaned against the bar with their backs to the rest of the Class of 1982. Much like when they were in High School, they were loners together. Jared wanted to be a part of the "In Crowd" and it killed him that he was so far out on the outside. Stitch, however, accepted his role in his social standing of high school. Sure he would have loved to have been a jock and wore a lettermen's jacket and dated cheerleaders and been the life of parties. But that wasn't meant to be. At least not until senior year, that is.

"Do you remember being in that play?" Jared said, as he swallowed down a gulp of his drink.

"OH YEAH!" Stitch replied as the fond memories came back to his mind. He remembered that it was a bad year for him at home and the senior play made everything seem just right.

It all started when his sister Caitlin had run away from home all because Leon had asked her to do the dishes. Caitlin freaked out and ran out of the house and moved in with her boyfriend and his parents who lived across the river. Gerti was devastated and Leon didn't know how to react. Caitlin was threatening to take her parents to court where she would petition to be an emancipated minor. If she succeeded, she would be able to collect her portion of Leon's Social Security Disability checks. Life was already a financial burden for the LeRue family and Caitlin's antics had only made matters worse. Stitch was just 17-years-old and wanted to help his parents as much as possible, but they didn't share much of what was happening at the time. Stitch only knew from what he had seen and what little he had overheard. Gerti stayed in her room, depressed and crying all the time while Leon sat in front of the television smoking cigarettes and drinking his coffee. It stayed like that for months until one day; Caitlin called and said she wanted to come home. Gerti was happy because it was around the holidays and she was pleased that her daughter would be home for Christmas. However, her happiness was cut short because just the day after Christmas Caitlin had taken her Christmas presents and moved back in with her boyfriend. Gerti retreated back to her sitting room with the door closed and Leon… well, nothing really changed with Leon. Coffee, cigarettes and television kept him occupied. Yelling at Stitch, Earl and Melanie was something that he did if the other three things were interrupted.

Jared had suggested that Stitch join the Drama club and audition for a role in 'South Pacific'. Jared got the part of Luther Billis and Stitch accepted the part of Lieutenant Joseph Cable. There was to be love scenes and kissing and singing and the girl who played Liat, his character's love interest, was a sophomore, but she was part of the 'Cheerleading clique'. Stitch was petrified of the idea of having to act like he was in love with someone who was part of the popular crowd. He was terrified of having to sing in front of his entire school. It was bad enough that they threw pencils at him and called him "geek-boy" and "scum-bag"; drama club would only ensure they'd have more ammo to throw at him. But Jared made it all sound fun and before Stitch knew it, he was cast for the role. So rather than going home and hearing how screwed up things were, he was able stay after school and rehearse for the play were he was able to practice his songs and learn his lines.

"I miss those days." Stitch said absently as he stared at the mirror behind the bar and gazed at the reflection of his old classmate's who suddenly morphed into their teenage counterparts. Instantly, he was standing in the auditorium of the Cohoes High School, watching his friend Jared rehears his scenes. Stitch laughed as Jared came out from behind the curtains wearing a coconut brazier with a mop wig and dancing in a grass skirt...

March 1982

Stitch sat in the audience seats and giggled at sight of his friend, Jared. The entire cast was in hysterics, but calmed down quickly as the song started up. As Stitch directed his attention back down to his script, he suddenly noticed someone standing to his left. He was sitting in the audience seats where there was a single light over his head. Aside from the stage, the rest of the auditorium looked as though it were cast in black satin so he had to squint into the dark to see who was at his side.

"Whaddaya doin'?" Asked a familiar voice.

"Learning my lines." Stitch replied to the darkness. "What's been going on with you?" Stitch tossed his script book to the side and stood up to greet his cousin Danielle. It had been a few years since she and Aunt Terri and Uncle Dan had moved from Cataract Street to

Van Schaick Island where they purchased a house and lived near a pond. It was still a part of Cohoes; however in the early days of the city's history, it was a country club for the wealthy. The Mohawk River cut through Cohoes and made several little islands and Van Schaick was the largest of the tiny islands and was converted to an exclusive community. However, as time passed, things changed and the island retained only its name and soon the status was gone. Uncle Dan had found a nice house for a great price and decided he couldn't pass it up so he moved Vince, Danielle and Aunt Terri away from Cataract Street and onto the island. It saddened Stitch when his cousins moved away. He missed his Aunt Terri and Uncle Dan very much and he especially missed his cousins Danielle and Vince. Even though Leon had so many other brothers and sisters, he was closest with Aunt Terri and Danielle and Vince. Not for any other reason but the fact that they lived so close for so long. He missed seeing them every day, and he was glad when High School started, so he could see his cousins during the week.

"I was wondering if you had a date for the prom." Danielle asked. Stitch thought it was kind of weird that his cousin would be asking him to the prom and he grew nervous.

"Uhm... I... Uh..." His eyes darted around the auditorium as he tried not to look his cousin in the face when he turned her down.

"Not for ME, Jerk-wad!" She said as she punched him in the arm. "One of my friends doesn't have a date and

I wanted to know if you would want to go with her?" She said.

Stitch looked past his cousin's shoulder and noticed a large silhouette in the doorway at the back of the auditorium. "Who's your *friend*?" He asked suspiciously.

"She's real nice." Danielle replied, avoiding her name.

"I'm sure she is." Stitch retorted with a furrowed brow. "But *who* is she?"

Danielle sighed in defeat. "Doreen Siphany." She said, looking away from Stitch.

"WHAT!" Stitch couldn't believe what he was hearing. Doreen was known as *blabbermouth* and it was justified. She could talk up a storm and never even stop for air. She wore huge glasses and talked louder then the schools P.A. system. The girl was as big as Sasquatch and almost as hairy!

Danielle shushed her cousin quickly. "She's standing at the door, she'll hear you!" Danielle said, trying to save Bigfoot from embarrassment. "Will you go with her?"

"No WAY!" Stitch whispered, taking his cousin's cue.

"Well who are you going with?" Danielle asked in a manner that was meant to prove a point.

"I ain't goin' at all!" Stitch replied.

"Why not?" Danielle asked with concern.

"Because I don't want to go." Stitch lied. "Prom is stupid!" Truth-be-told He did want to go, but he didn't need a pity date from his cousin's *shaved beast* of a friend and he knew his parents couldn't afford to rent him a tuxedo or buy a corsage for his date. He already felt stupid going to the Class Ring Dinner even though he wasn't able to afford a class ring. The embarrassment just wasn't worth it. After all, he'd seen "Carrie", and he wasn't about to be the victim of this school's Prom Pranks.

"Why would anyone not want to go to their prom?" Danielle asked. "It's going to be the best night of our lives!"

"Maybe for you." Stitch said as he plopped back into his seat and picked up his script. "But for me, the prom is stupid and I don't wanna go."

"You mean, you don't wanna go with *Doreen.*" Danielle accused.

"No." Stitch replied as he opened the pages of his script. "I don't wanna go *at all.*" He turned his attention to his pages and pretended to read as his cousin stood there; steaming with anger. When she finally stormed off, Stitch threw his script pages against the seat in front of him and sank back with frustration. He was angry with Danielle for bringing the subject up and he was upset with his parents for being broke and he was upset with his sister for making the situation even worse. Stitch closed his eyes, took a deep breath and exhaled with the hopes that everything would be better soon.

"I remember Doreen." Jared said as he crushed his cigarette into the ashtray on the bar. "She was some congressmen's niece or something like that, right?"

"I guess." Stitch replied plainly.

"Holy Shit, dude!" Jared said. "Imagine if you went with her! She'd be gabbing the entire time you were trying to bang her!" Jared laughed so loud other people at the bar looked over his way.

Stitch leaned in and tried to silence his friend. "She's not someone I would *'bang'*, Jared."

"Yeah, only *Tami Foxxer* is privileged for that, eh?" Jared said with a smirk.

DECEMBER 1980

It was Christmas and rather than snow, it was raining outside. Stitch was at a Christmas party with his parents and his mom's sister, Percy. Stitch felt a particular closeness with his Aunt Percy and enjoyed being around her. She was Gerti's younger sister and she was married to her second husband, Patrick. It was Patrick's family that was throwing the Christmas Party and Stitch didn't really know anyone except for his cousin Bailey, who was out in the rain Christmas Caroling with Stitch's brother, Earl, and some other kids. Stitch came back in from caroling and took off his wet jacket and sweater and went over to sit between his mother and his Aunt Percy who were sharing a bottle of wine. They talked over Stitch's head while drinking from the bottle as they passed it in front of him. Stitch wasn't listening to their conversation; he just enjoyed being close to them. His mother was more like a big sister at this point in his life. She would joke with him and the two of them would tease and torment Leon just for the fun of it. As the two sisters drank wine and talked, Stitch watched his father interact with Patrick and Patrick's family. Leon's once, jet-black hair was now salt-n-peppered with flecks of gray. He no longer wore the green khakis that he wore when he worked in the mills. Now he wore slacks with flannel shirts and the sleeves rolled up. From across the room, Stitch could still see the veins protruding from his father's hands. He thought about how much his father had been through over the years and how strong of a man he had to be to put up with everything life had dealt him.

A loud crack sound accompanied by a short stinging burn in the back of his head took his attention away from his father and he looked at his mother, who was sitting on the side of him that suddenly hurt. "What was that for?" He asked as he rubbed the feeling in the back of his head."

"Ah dind do it." His mother slurred. He felt the smack again and he realized it was his Aunt Percy who's arm was behind the back of couch. She was sitting sideways, with her arm behind him. He turned to her with a curious look and was about to ask her why she hit him in the head, but she beat him to it.

"I was talking to you, ya friggin' idiot." She said with a laugh. "I asked you if you've been laid yet!"

Stitch turned his head to face his mother and then turned towards his aunt and then again back to his mother. He didn't know how to answer her question. He didn't want sound like a '*wuss*' but he didn't know how his mother would react if she knew he was having sex. The only thing Stitch could think to do was to shrug his shoulders and say nothing.

"Whaddaya' mean you don't know?" Percy squawked. "How could you not know if you've been laid or not?"

"Here." His mother said as she thrust the bottle of wine in front of him. "Drink this." She said.

Stitch felt like he was being set up and declined with a polite smile and a wave of the hand.

"Drink it." She said, pushing it closer to him. "You're sixteen, it's ok." She placed it in his hands. "G'head, it's all right."

Stitch brought the bottle up to his lips and tipped up the bottle, all the while keeping his eye on his mother for a look of disapproval. When she smiled, he drank. The liquid was dry and didn't taste anything like he thought it would. But he liked it nonetheless. After several sips – more like gulps – of the wine, and constant prodding of his sex-life from his Aunt Percy, Stitch finally admitted that he was still a virgin. Every head in the room was looking at him as he realized that he had made that statement a little louder than necessary. His eyes swiveled in their sockets and his brain sloshed in his skull. Rather than be embarrassed, he laughed out loud, bringing his Aunt and his mother into hysterics with him. As their laughter died down, Gerti took a hold of the lapel on Stitch's shirt and pulled him close to her face and gave her son some '*motherly advice*'.

"You see that guy over there?" Gerti said as she pointed to his father, Leon. As Stitch nodded, she continued. "If you want to have any success with women, then don't be anything like *him*!" She took another sip of the wine and handed it to her son who took a large gulp. He could feel the warmth of the dry liquid as it coated his throat and worked its way into his belly. "That man has no goddamned emotions." She stated. Her green eyes looked up at Leon, as she spoke, never letting go of her son's shirt. "You have to be gentle with a woman. You have to care for her and love her. You have to treat a woman as though she's your Queen." Gerti sat and held her son's shirt while staring intently at her husband. When she slightly swayed to the tune of alcohol in her brain, she let go of Stitch's shirt and padded it flat with the palm of her hand. "Never take a woman for granted and don't ever make her feel as though she's not worth your love. Even if she's just a one-night-stand, or a quickie you should make her feel like she's the only woman in the world." Gerti's eyes met her son's eyes. Both of them were cock-eyed but every word she spoke was sinking into her son's head. "Ya' got that?"

Stitch nodded his understanding and then looked back at his father. His mind wandered back to the day he had seen his parents together in his father's hospital room. The lack of emotion between his parents made Stitch try to recall if he had ever seen any type of affection between the two of them. He could only count a handful of time he'd seen them hug or kiss. As he soaked in his mother's words, his Aunt Percy leaned in and whispered in his other ear.

"And be sure they cum before you do!" She slurred with the breath of wine.

Stitch slowly turned his face to his Aunt's who had the most serious and sincere look. After a few seconds of regarding each other's looks, the three of them broke out into a large, loud, drunken laugh.

Stitch couldn't remember the rest of that night, except for singing *Feliz Navidad* on the ride back home.

"I don't know how you had so many friggin' women." Jared said as he signaled the bartender to refill their glasses. "What the hell was your secret with the girls anyhow?"

Stitch smiled, took a long drag off his cigarette and looked Jared in the eye as he recited his advice for women. "I treat them like queens and make sure they cum before I do."

The two friends looked at one another for a long moment and then burst into laughter as they clicked their glasses together.

"To Cumming Second!" Jared Saluted as he raised his glass.

"To Cumming Second!" Stitch repeated, toasting his friend.

The two friends drank and laughed and recalled their Senior Year of High School as the best year. They became the most popular guys at the Skating Arena, since they'd been going there for a few years. The two of them would go there every Friday and Saturday Night and would never pay a dime to get in. Girls would actually skate around the arena collecting change from other girls to gather up enough money to get the two of them into the rink. Every five or ten minutes a girl would come by with a handful of change and pour it into Stitch or Jared's hands and skate away to collect more. Jared and Stitch would count it and even though they had enough to rent skates and pay admission, they would tell the girls, "Just fifty cents more!!" and the girls would roll away to collect more money for the dynamic duo. Each of them would come back with another fifty cents and Stitch and Jared would have enough to play pinball and buy drinks and pretzels and whatever else...

After skating for a few hours, Stitch and Jared turned in their skates and walked into the disco where they were well known. They could have had any girl in the place and they both knew it. One girl, in particular, caught Stitch's eye. She had curly, auburn hair and the most amazing eyes. She was a few months younger than Stitch, but she looked like she was much older. *At least nineteen!* Stitch thought when he'd seen her. She was gorgeous and Stitch knew he had to make her his girlfriend. However, he walked up to her, the way he walked up to most girls in that place. However, he was about to find out that she wasn't like most girls from that place. He strode up slowly, with his hands in the pockets of his tight fitting jeans and he smiled at her and looked his baby blues directly into her deep, sapphire eyes. "Hey." He said with a slight nod and nothing more.

"Hey." She replied casually. She might not have shown that she was impressed, but Stitch was sure that she was, even if only in his mind.

"I'm Stitch." He said as he tossed his hair back out of his face.

"Yeah. I know." She said. Stitch looked over at Jared and winked, letting him know how confident he was that this was going well. However, Jared's eyes widened, signaling Stitch that something was wrong. When Stitch turned back around, the girl was gone.

"Well I'll be a son-of-a-bitch!" Stitch said to himself as he walked back to his friends.

"Oooh!" Jared said mockingly. "You sure showed her!"

"Screw you." Stitch plopped down on the seat in the corner. It was a large, cable spool, covered in carpet. He looked around the room, trying to find where this beautiful girl went but the flashing lights combined with the loud music and crowded dance floor made it impossible. Stitch tapped Jared on the shoulder to let him know he was going to the café for something to drink. As Stitch strode through the Arcade, he noticed her again. She was standing by a Zaxxon machine talking to another girl. Stitch realized he might have come on a little strong and walked up to her again. However, this time he did so with a bit of humility in his manner.

"Excuse me." He said sheepishly. "I didn't mean to be a jerk back there." He said as he pointed his thumb over his shoulder toward the disco. "I just wanted to know your name and ask you if I could have the next slow dance."

She smiled at him this time and seemed more like she was interested in what he had to say. "It's Tami." She said with a smile. "Tami Foxxer".

Stitch offered his hand as he told her his name again. "Stitch LeRue." He said. She reached out and touched his hand and told him it was a pleasure to meet him. But Stitch didn't hear a word she said. Her touch had him mesmerized as he heard birds singing in his head. His ears grew hot and his face flushed warm. It suddenly seemed as though the entire arcade grew twenty degrees warmer and Stitch could feel sweat rolling down his back. He found that he couldn't take his eyes from her face. She had the most beautiful skin, like that of a porcelain doll. Her hair was perfect with not a strand out of place. Never had he seen such beauty or been so close to it. Suddenly, Stitch realized the look on her face was as if he had suddenly started growing a second or something. *Oh my god, she said something and I didn't hear her!*

"I'm sorry." He said quickly, thinking of a good excuse for not hearing her. "These pinball machines are so loud." He said. *And your beauty is captivating!* He thought.

"I said they're playing a slow song if you want to dance now." She pointed in the direction of the disco.

"Ok." Stitch replied quickly. He nearly dragged her into the disco and onto the floor so that he could get as much dance time as possible. As the two danced, Stitch could feel the warmth of her body against his. Her firm, ample breasts were pushing into his abdomen and her hair was just under his nose. It smelled like apple blossoms and her body felt like heaven in his arms. He stood tall as he swayed to the music with her. He wanted everyone on the floor to see him dancing with the most beautiful girl in the building. *In the State! IN THE WORLD!*

As he looked up, he noticed his friend, the DJ, giving him the 'thumbs up' sign and Stitch smiled as he raised two fingers with a pleading look on his face. His friend smiled and nodded acknowledgement, knowing that Stitch wanted him to play a second slow dance song. Moments later, the song started to fade out and everyone on the floor was breaking off from their partner, but Stitch pulled Tami closer and whispered in her ear, "The DJ is a friend of mine. He's going to play another one for us."

She looked up at him and smiled. "Hmmm. A man of power." She said sarcastically. "That's *very* impressive."

She giggled as she placed her head against this chest again and the two swayed slowly to the music.

As Stitch and Jared walked from the skating arena to Jared's house, they talked about the night.

"Did you get her number?" Jared asked.

"Yepper!" Stitch replied with a wide smile.

"Didn't your mom have your phone turned off this year again?" Jared reminded him.

"Not a problem." Stitch said. Jared didn't know it, but after the first time Stitch's mother had the phone turned off, he found a payphone near a drug store in the city and he memorized the number and would tell girls to call him at that phone at a specific time. To make sure he would get his calls, he took the *'DO NOT USE'* sign off of a soda vending machine and taped it to the payphone to make sure no one else would use it. Every evening, after dinner, Stitch would make the twenty-minute walk to the downtown area and sit next to the phone and wait for his phone calls. He would only have to do this for another month as his mother promised him they would have the phone turned back on.

"This is the greatest!" Stitch said as he tucked Tami's number into his pocket. "I really love that place!" He said, referring to the skating arena.

"I know." Jared replied. "I can't wait until next Friday." Jared had met a girl as well. Her name was Toni and he was crazy about her. However, Toni only went to the arena on Friday evenings, whereas Stitch and Jared went every Friday and Saturday Night.

"Do you think it will be like this when we're in the Navy?" Stitch asked.

"Whaddaya mean?"

"You and me." Stitch said. "Do you think we'll still be friends like this?"

"Dude!" Jared said as he stopped walking. He seemed surprised by Stitch's question. "We'll always be friends. Nothing will ever change that." Jared reached out and flicked Stitch on the tip of his nose again, showing his annoyance with such a silly question.

"I know." Stitch said as he started walking again. "But do you think it will be like *this*?" He emphasized the final word by spreading his arms wide and looking up at the starry sky. "This is so great! I mean, everything seems so 'right' for us right now. I only wish Arnold was here to share it with us, you know what I mean."

"I know." Jared replied. " The two remained quiet for a moment of respect before Jared broke out singing "Bloody Mary" from the Musical they were in. "And you get to make out with Pam Riley!" Jared said as he punched Stitch in the arm. With the role of Lt. Cables, Stitch's character is one who falls in love with Liat, the Polynesian islander girl. However, Pam Riley isn't just any ordinary girl. She was a sophomore, but she was smoking hot. Her hair was long and black and her skin was tanned bronze. She looked like a Polynesian islander girl and Stitch had a love scene with her.

"Dude! She is SO, Freakin' HOT!" Stitch said.

"Are you really gonna kiss her?" Jared asked.

"I have to, man." Stitch said emphatically. "For the good of the production, I wouldn't do any less!"

The two boys laughed hysterically and soon began signing more songs from their production, all the while walking down Route 9R at eleven o'clock at night.

"We were a couple of geeks, eh?" Stitch said as he drank down his drink. But Jared didn't hear him. His attention was turned to something behind Stitch.

"Who is that?" Jared asked in a soft voice of wonder.

Stitch slowly turned around and looked in the direction of Jared's gaze and immediately recognized the beautiful woman who walked into the lodge. Her hair was done up and she was wearing a magnificent gown with a slit in the front that showed off her amazing legs as she walked over to the sign-in table. She took a "Hello" tag and put it in her purse, rather than sticking it to her dress. She looked around the hall as if she were looking for someone specific. She noticed Stitch and waved to him and did her best to hold her smile. Stitch stood up from the bar and straightened his jacket and waved back. He knew it took a lot of courage for Marge to come to the reunion and he wanted to make sure she didn't regret it.

Stitch reached out and flicked Jared on the tip of his nose as he told him, "Mind your manners, young man."

"Dude!" Jared's eyes followed the attractive woman through the room. "What *is* it with you?" Jared said as he stood up from the bar and followed Stitch. "Who is she?"

"You wouldn't believe me if I told you." Stitch replied. Before Jared could question him further, Stitch walked away and met her in the middle of the room and greeted her with a hug. The two walked back towards the bar, arm in arm where Stitch introduced her to Jared.

"Jared, this is Marge Collington." He said plainly, hoping that Jared wouldn't immediately think of her as 'Large Marge'. "Marge, this is Jared Cormier. Stitch elbowed Jared, when he noticed his friend's mouth was hanging open.

"Marge Collington?" He asked curiously. "You were in our class?" Jared couldn't recall the name right off the bat and he crossed his arms over his chest as he gave her a serious once over.

"For a while." She replied. "But I graduated High School in Florida."

"Marge Collington..." Jared repeated, trying to place a face to the name.

Stitch could almost see Jared's brain twisting and turning as he tried to figure out who she used to be. Stitch didn't want to use her nickname to jar his memory, although it would probably work best, however Marge beat him to it.

"Just try to remember, *Large Marge*." She said plainly.

It was as if Jared had an epiphany. His eyes lit up and he smiled widely. "YOU'RE LARGE MARGE?" He said, pointing to her and making a spectacle of himself.

"Dude!" Stitch said, trying to calm him down. "Chill!"

Realizing he was being too loud, Jared lowered his voice and leaned in and shook her hand. "Oh my god, you look amazing!" He said with a laugh. "You're not *fat* anymore!" Jared was never one to harness his thoughts. If he had something to say, he just said it.

Stitch felt embarrassed for her, but she just laughed and told him time was good to her.

"You can say that again, sister!" Jared said as he slapped his own knee. "Wow!"

"You'll have to forgive him." Stitch said smiling. "He's a bit shy when it comes to meeting people." His tone was friendly, but the sarcasm was definitely noted.

"I'm sure he'll warm up eventually." Marge said with a giggle.

Stitch smiled as he realized she was able to take his cue and keep the joke going. It was as if she knew what he was thinking and she reacted to it. Jared smiled as he noticed her quick wit and responded, "She's good!" while pointing his finger in her direction. "Lemme buy you a drink!"

As the new friends stood at the bar and drank, neither of them said a single word. The three of them simply stood at the bar with their eyes focused on the various bottles that lined the wall, behind the bar. They remained as such for nearly five minutes before Jared broke the silence and announced his need to urinate. Actually, his words were, "I gotta go drain the main vein!"

"Such the eloquent speaker." Stitch smiled as he watched his friend head off to the men's room.

"The two of you have been friends for a long time." Marge said as she placed her glass on the bar. "It must be nice to have a friend like that."

Stitch took a moment to regard her words before responding. "It's definitely been an experience."

Marge was about to ask him what he meant, but knew he was holding back for a reason and decided not to pry. Before she could ask him anything more about it, the two of them were interrupted with a familiar face.

"Hey, remember me?" asked a short, stocky woman. Stitch looked at her and then looked to Marge for help; however, the blank look on Marge's face told Stitch that she was no closer to an answer than he was. Stitch's eyes quickly scanned her thick body in the hopes of seeing a nametag but came up empty. "Ellen!" She shouted with excitement. "Ellen Kravich!"

Even though the name was familiar to Stitch he had no memory of being in any of her classes.

To avoid being rude, he gave a look of surprise and exclaimed, "Wow! How have you been?"

"I'm good!" She replied with a large smile. "Is this your wife?" Ellen asked as she held her hand out to Marge.

"No." Marge replied with a polite smile. "We're just friends."

"I didn't think you were in our class." Ellen said, as she looked her up and down. "At first you didn't look familiar to me. But now..." Ellen gave a perplexed look as she gazed at Marge, trying to place her, but Stitch jumped in and led Ellen away.

"She's actually from Florida." Stitch said. "You may remember her from our elementary school days." Stitch said. Marge's eyes now looked worried, but Stitch gave her a glance of confidence.

"You went to elementary school with us?" Ellen asked.

"Yes. Replied Marge with a bit of a smile. "As a matter of fact, you sat in front of me in the fifth grade."

"Oh, that's nonsense." Ellen replied. "The girl who sat behind me was..." Ellen stopped when she noticed the look on Stitch's face.

She did a double take as she looked closer at Marge's face and suddenly Ellen's face became flushed crimson. "Marge Collington?" Ellen seemed shocked.

"In the flesh." Marge replied with a bit of a nervous tone.

"More like HALF the flesh!" Ellen laughed, remarking how much weight Marge had lost. "Wow! You look amazing!"

"Thank you." Marge replied. Stitch smiled as he noticed that Marge did not return the compliment to Ellen. For years and years all the kids at the school were mean and cruel to her; literally forcing her and her family to move way. It was her time to shine and Stitch couldn't have been happier for her.

As the night wore on, Stitch realized his reason for wanting to come to the reunion was insignificant. Stitch had something change in his life and he wanted to return home and rub it into the faces of those who made him feel invisible and worthless. However, as he learned more and more about his former classmates, he came to realize that the mean, nasty kids from so many years ago were no longer a threat to him. They were no longer around and he would only be doing himself an injustice by carrying out his plan. He was satisfied with the way things were and happy to know that even the meanest of the kids from his school had become real people and moved past the type of persons they were as teenagers. Stitch decided this would be the time to leave and not come back; at least not until the 50th Class Reunion, because by then, most of his classmates would be too old to show up. Stitch walked over to Jared and told him he needed to be leaving; however, Jared tried to protest.

"It's not that I don't enjoy seeing you, I really do." Stitch told Jared as he placed his hand on his friend's shoulder. "It's just that being here is not fun for me. These people aren't who the used to be when we were in school, and now I just feel like I don't belong."

"C'mon, Dude!" Jared pleaded. His eyes were half open and he was spilling his drink as he tried to stand up from his chair. "Don't let these friggin' idiots ruin a good night for us!"

"Really, it's okay." Stitch replied. "Besides, I have an early flight back to Pittsburgh in the morning."

"Yer not goin' to the pancake breakfast?" Jared sounded shocked, as if he had just received news that the world was about to end.

Stitch smiled at his life long friend and he pulled him close and hugged him. "I love you, bro." Stitch said over Jared's shoulder. "You mean the world to me, and if I could stay, I would."

"It's cool." Jared said as he returned the hug. "Keep in touch, man."

Stitch let go of his friend and stood back as he regarded Jared for a moment. He told Jared to take care of himself and then exited the room quickly. Before heading past a crowd that stood near the main entrance, Stitch ducked into the men's room and took cover in a stall as he felt a sting in his eyes that were tear-ing up. He didn't want anyone to see him like crying and the bathroom was his only option. As the door to the stall closed, the floodgates to his eyes opened and Stitch quietly sobbed for a moment. So many years he had lost with Jared and he'd never get them back. He missed his best friend, but seeing him made Stitch realize just how much he missed being a young man with him.

After refreshing himself, Stitch left the men's room and found Marge standing in a corner near the main entrance. Her arms were crossed over her chest and there was a playful look of annoyance in her eye.

"You weren't thinking of ducking out on me, were you?" She said as she moved in his direction. Knowing that Stitch was wondering how she found out, Marge let him know, "Jared told me to try and stop you."

Stitch spread his arms as he tried to come up with a polite answer only to let them fall back to his side in defeat as he nodded yes. "It's been nice meeting you and spending time with you, but I really need to get out of here."

"Oh, *YOU* need to get out of here?" Marge's tone was sarcastic and Stitch suddenly realized that if anyone had a reason to leave the reunion, it was Marge Collington.

"You got me." Stitch smiled. "I thought it would be less painful if I just disappeared with out a trace."

"Wrong answer, bud." Marge's eyes were smiling again. "How about we go to the 76 diner and you can make up for it by buying me a cup of coffee."

Without hesitation Stitch replied with a large smile, "Absolutely."

CHAPTER TEN

Stitch had only been to the 76 Diner a few times with his father, but he'd heard all about the place from other kids when he was in the school. Most of the kids would go out partying on a Friday or Saturday night and before going home, they would meet up at the 76 to drink coffee, or order breakfast as a way to sober up before going back home. It was the place for all those cliques, who were interactive and social with one another; but it was not a place for kids like Stitch and Marge. The 76 Diner was a 'greasy-spoon' that had long been a tradition for rowdy teenagers since its inception and on this particular night, it seemed ironic that two misfits, like that of Stitch and Marge, would take refuge in the one place they would never have been welcomed as teenagers. As they sat in a booth against the window, waiting for their waitress to take their orders, Stitch observed a group of fifteen and sixteen year olds as they sat down at the far end of the diner. They were taking up three booths and were being loud and obnoxious. Stitch tried to imagine his classmates sitting there and carrying on like that and was almost glad he'd never taken part in such a ritual. Marge wondered how many of those kids were the children of her former classmates who were still standing in clique circles at the Elks Lodge along the bank of the Mohawk River in Cohoes. Just before deciding to go some place quieter and with quicker service, an older waitress approached their table. Her silver hair was a tousled mess and she looked like she'd been through the gauntlet.

"I swear to god!" She said as she pulled out a pad from the apron tied around her stocky waist and flipped up a few pages. "I've been working here for thirty years, and these kids just keep getting worse and worse!" Stitch smiled at the woman's comment, but she didn't notice as she checked her left ear and then found the pencil she was looking for behind her right ear. "What can I get for you folks?" She asked as she stood ready to take their order.

The two new friends ordered breakfast and sat patiently, waiting for their food. The conversation was practically nil when Marge decided it was time to end the silence.

"If you'd have told me, twenty-five years ago, that the two of us would be sitting in the 76 diner having breakfast together, I would have said you were crazy!"

They laughed at Marge's comment and soon the conversation flowed smoothly. They talked about their lives after school and Stitch learned a lot about his new friend. Some of the things he learned made him smile, while other things caused him to want to look away and pretend he didn't hear what she'd said. When Stitch spoke, he talked about his years in the Navy and how he was medically discharged and forced back into the civilian world. He spoke proudly of his time served and they laughed at his stories of the different countries he visited and the different types of trouble he got into while visiting those countries. He told her about his life in Pittsburgh and a situation that nearly left him for dead. He'd never shared these stories with anyone and he wasn't sure if it was the fact that he might never see Marge again, or the fact that he actually felt comfortable enough telling her his stories' but it certainly felt good to talk about it. Speaking to her had a therapeutic benefit that he appreciated.

After nearly an hour of talking and laughing, and some crying; the two new friends never even noticed the group of kids in the corner of the diner any longer. Every now and again, their waitress would come over and refill Marge's coffee cup or she would give Stitch a new tea bag and fresh hot water with lemon; but that was the only interruption the two ever had.

Marge smiled when the conversation dwindled down and then glanced at the clock on the wall above Stitch's head. "I hadn't realized it was so late." She said with a sad tone to her voice as she noticed it was approaching 2am.

"I guess you probably have to get back to your nephew." Stitch said as a way to let her know he understood if she needed to end their night.

"The sitter wouldn't mind the extra pay." Marge said with a soft smile. "But I really should be getting home."

Stitch and Marge finished their breakfasts and paid their bill before they exchanged phone numbers, emails and instant message screen names. They promised to stay in touch with one another once Stitch returned to Pittsburgh.

"Kinda' hard to NOT stay in touch these days." Stitch said with a smile as he waved

all of her electronic information between his fingers.

Stitch made sure Marge made it safely back to her apartment before he returned to his hotel room and packed up his small bag for the next day's trip

Albany County Airport hadn't changed all that much in the years since Stitch was last there. It was still very small and very quaint. Despite its petite size for an airport, it was classified as an "International Airport", but only because it made a few trips to Canada, which was just a quick jog to the corner for an airline pilot out of Albany. As Stitch checked his bag, something familiar struck him as he approached his gate.

CHAPTER ELEVEN

August 2nd, 1982

Stitch sat in the living room and watched the new Paul McCartney and Stevie Wonder video, Ebony and Ivory on MTV. As he sat and watched, it hadn't really dawned on him that the past eleven months had all led up to this point in his life.

At the beginning of the school year, Jared and Stitch were walking through the Latham Circle Mall, as they did every weekend. They liked to hang out there before going to the skating rink. Jared was a master at the video game DEFENDERS and would log hundreds of hours on the game and getting the high score came easy for him. Stitch, on the other hand, was a pinball fanatic and enjoyed playing one pinball machine, in particular; BLACK KNIGHT. He would get free games, and hit specials all day long. Stitch and Jared would cruise the mall early in the afternoon looking for friends from the skating rink and soon the entire gang would be patrolling the mall. However, on this particular September weekend, Stitch and Jared were on their usual route of the mall when Jared pointed out a U.S. Navy recruiter's sign and joked about the childhood dream they shared.

"Remember how we used to want to join the Navy and get stationed on an aircraft carrier off the coast of Japan?" Jared laughed.

"Yeah, I remember." Stitch replied. Only, Stitch wasn't laughing. He stood there looking dumbstruck and staring at the poster of the sailor holding a little boy's hand as they gazed out at a ship in the harbor. Stitch immediately thought about Arnold and how joining the Navy was his dream too, except it was too late for Arnold. He had moved to Florida where died of Leukemia and Stitch and Jared were never able to see him again. Not even for his funeral.

"What's up, man?" Jared asked as he noticed his friend was staring intently at the sign.

"Dude! Where are you going to college?" Stitch said, trying to prove a point.

"Fuck that!" Jared replied. "Once I finish this senior year, I ain't ever going back to school!"

"So where are you gonna work?" Stitch was setting up his chess pieces and was about to make checkmate in two moves!

Jared shrugged. "I dunno." He thought for a moment. "Probably get a job at the firehouse with my dad, or maybe in the mills. Why?"

Stitch reached up and flicked Jared on the tip of his nose trying to get his point across. "Like my cousin, Vince?" Stitch reminded Jared. Two years earlier, Vince had fallen down an elevator shaft and damaged his neck and back while working in the mills. He was laid up for months. When Vince tried to go into the Navy, they wouldn't take him when it was time to go. "Is that how you want to end up?"

Jared thought about it for a moment. "That was a freak accident." Jared said in defense of the mills. Jared knew he didn't want to work in the mills, but he also knew he didn't want to go to college. "What's your point, Man?"

Stitch literally grabbed the back of Jared's head and turned his eyes to the recruiter's poster. "Why don't we do it?"

Jared was shocked. "You mean *actually* join the Navy?"

"Why not?" Stitch said with a purpose. "We're seniors this year!"

"I never did take my SAT's" Jared mumbled to himself.

With only a little prodding from Stitch, Jared agreed and the two walked into that recruiter's office as teen-aged boys, but came out feeling like American Men. They had signed up for the Navy and they had even sworn in! The only thing they needed was to have their parents sign off on the contract since they weren't eighteen yet and neither of them had any problem getting their parents to agree to letting them go into the Navy.

All through school, they bragged how they'd signed up on the Delayed Entry Program, and Stitch even started signing his name as *S. LeRue, E-1, USN*, on all his homework assignments and tests.

When Stitch and Jared joined the Drama club and were in the production of South Pacific; and Stitch was a bit jealous that Jared played the part of a sailor, while he had to play the part of a Marine Corps Officer.

The senior year flew by and graduation was a blast! Stitch's parents allowed him to have a party at his house with beer and food. It was an amazing time for the two of them. All of Stitch's friends from the drama club showed up. There had to have been more than a hundred kids at the house. Leon purchased two or three beer balls and told the kids to stay in the house and back yard and to not leave the premises without an adult. Stitch was surprised how everyone complied and did as requested. Stitch and his friends drank until they were thoroughly drunk, (which was not so hard for an 18-year-old Stitch), and it was only then that the party got better. Mikey Turnball, a guy from the production crew, passed out in the living room and the rest of the guys at the party took a marker and drew roadmaps all over his chest, back and face! In the kitchen, Leon was cooking frozen pizzas, but the kids were eating them so fast, that he placed two in the oven and then cooked two more in skillets on the stovetop! Stitch and Jared felt as though they were finally '*somebody*' in their school. Even if only to a small group of people who belonged to a drama club, it was enough for them. It may have come four years too late, but at least it came! Finally they had made a name for themselves and soon would be heading off to the Navy.

It was 4:30 in the morning and Stitch's mother knocked on his bedroom door to wake him up. She had packed him a small bag with razor blades and deodorant and some new underwear that she had purchased at Fishermen's for him. Once fully dressed, Stitch took the bag his mother packed for him and went downstairs to the living room to wait for his recruiter to come take him away to his new life. The bookshelves, in the living room, were bare and most of the things were packed up. Stitch's parents were planning on moving to California with Gerti's sister, Percy, who had moved out there months earlier. After much debate Gerti was finally able to convinced Leon to move against his better judgment. Caitlin was still living in Troy with her boyfriend and had dropped out of school and Stitch was leaving for the Navy, so Gerti thought it was the perfect time to move the rest of the family across country.

"You want something to eat before you leave?" Gerti asked her son.

"No thanks." Stitch replied, as he watched MTV and waited for his ride.

"Just have a bowl of cereal or something." Gerti said, worried that her son might not eat for quite some time.

"No. Thank You." This time Stitch emphasized each word, trying to get his point across to his mother. Looking back, he wasn't sure if it was him being nervous about leaving, or if he was actually annoyed, but he spoke out "That's one thing I won't miss." Stitch muttered, thinking his mother couldn't hear him. "That nasty friggin' Carnation Instant Milk!"

"Excuse me?" Gerti said with anger in her voice. "If you have something to say, young man, you say it to my face!"

Stitch was feeling brave. After all, he was eighteen years old and was about to go into the Navy. He didn't need to fear his mother any longer. As a matter of fact, he was more than a foot taller than she was, so he decided to stand up (literally) to his mother. He rose up from the sofa and repeated what he said, "I said I wouldn't miss that nasty, friggin, Carnation Instant Milk!" His tone was loud and he was pretty sure he got his point across as he walked towards the dining room. However, that childhood fear settled in when he heard his mother's foot falls as she stomped her way into the dining room. He was relieved to see there was no belt in her hands as she emerged from the Kitchen, however, she was able to grab the collar of his shirt and pick him up off the floor while slamming his back against the wall.

"You may be taller than me, mother-fucker, but I'm still your goddamned mother!"

Stitch couldn't believe that his toes wouldn't touch the floor when he tried pointing them downward. For a short woman, she was able to lift his skinny ass a good foot off of the floor!

"Do you understand me?" Gerti spoke through gritted teeth. Her face was nearly as red as her hair and all Stitch could do was nod yes as he held both his hands over the fist that balled up his shirt and pinned him to the wall. Slowly, Gerti let her son back down to the floor. "Your father and I did the best we could for you kids! We cut corners and probably did things that most parents wouldn't do, but we did them for the good of this family." Gerti was visibly upset, but not just by her thoughtless son's comments. She was upset by the fact that her daughter was still gone and that her son was going off to the military and that she still had two more kids at home to take care of and they were upset about leaving home and moving to California. Gerti took a breath and pulled it all in as best as she could. She certainly didn't want Stitch leaving home worried.

Stitch started to understand the sacrifices his parents had made for them. He suddenly understood why the phone and electricity were turned off in the summer seasons and why they sometimes mixed instant milk with regular milk. Sometimes, they would just mix the instant milk with water! Money was tight and if they couldn't split a gallon of milk into two, they would just make their own gallon of milk. It was horrible tasting, but it served its purpose. "I'm sorry, Mom." Stitch said as he found a new appreciation for all his parents did for him and the family.

Gerti said nothing. Instead, she used her hands to iron out the wrinkles she had made on his shirt and then walked away. No sooner than that was there a knock at the door. Stitch's heart skipped a beat as he realized his life was about to change. He opened the door to find Jared standing on the top step, just outside the kitchen door with their recruiter standing behind him.

"Say your good-bye's now, it's going to be about 10 hours before you see them again." The recruiter informed Stitch of the long entrance process at the AFEES building.

"Leon! Earl! Melanie!" Gerti called Stitch's father, brother, and baby sister down to say goodbye to him before he left for the AFEEs building, where he would be processed for the Navy. Earl gave Stitch a 'high-five' and Melanie gave him a hug. "I'll make you a necklace." She said as she let him go.

"I'd like that very much." Stitch said as he patted his baby sister on the head. Melanie was the love of his life and it pained him that he would miss her growing up by being in the Navy.

Stitch was approached by his father and wanted to hug him; however, he knew how his dad felt about that kind of thing. Instead Stitch held out his hand, knowing how his father felt about boys showing affection to one another. Leon regarded his son's gesture for a moment and took Stitch's hand and pulled him in close and gave him a hug. A tear formed up in Stitch's eye as he remembered the last time he hugged his father was nearly six years earlier when he was brought home from his trip to St. Coleman's home. "We'll see you at the airport, son." Was all his father was able to get out before his voice cracked.

Stitch turned to his mother and gave her a giant hug and a kiss on the cheek. "I love you, mom." He said. And then he whispered in her ear, "I'm sorry." Before Gerti could respond, the recruiter informed Stitch they were running behind and he could see them all at the airport before he left for Boot Camp. Stitch stepped back from his mother and took one last moment to regard his family and the house he grew up in before he turned and left that home forever.

The AFEEs building was packed with young men who were getting processed for the Military. Some were heading to the Army, others to the Marine Corps and Air Force while Stitch, Jared and a group of local boys were getting ready for the Navy. It was here that Jared and Stitch ran into Marty Coles, a guy they knew from the skating arena. The three boys had all known one another from skating, but none of them ever mentioned going into the Navy. Stitch thought it would be exciting that the three of them would possibly be going through boot camp together!

As the day dragged on with shots, and pokes and prods, Stitch started to regret turning down a bowl of Wheaties and instant milk and water. He was starving, and his six foot one inch, one hundred and eighteen pound body couldn't tolerate going much longer without food.

"We've been here, walking around in our underwear for more than five hours!" Stitch said with frustration. "When the hell are we gonna eat?"

"Not much longer." Marty replied. "I over heard them saying that we're supposed to get lunch vouchers to eat for free in the buildings cafeteria."

"I just hope they give us our pants back!" Jared said. He meant it to be serious, but it came out sounding quite funny to Stitch and Marty.

It was close to 4pm when all the new recruits were brought to the Albany County Airport where they were to fly out to their boot camp destinations. Stitch, Jared and Marty started looking for their families. Marty found his family and immediately took off to be with them. Stitch and Jared's family were standing together in a large group waving them over. As the two boys approached, they noticed a huge group of kids standing behind their families. It was the gang from the skating arena and they were all holding up a sheet, which they painted with the message, GOOD LUCK STITCH AND JARED! Around the boarders of the sheet, they had all signed their names. Most of them were girls and they put hearts and arrows with their names. It warmed the two of them to see all their friends wishing them off on a safe trip.

Out from the crowd of kids came Tamara Foxxer, with a small radio and cassette player. She put the radio on the floor and pressed the play button to a preset STYX song.

"Do you remember this song?" Tamara asked as she played "SAIL AWAY".

"That was the first song we slow danced to." Stitch replied with a smile.

Tamara took his hand and placed them on her hips. "For my sailor. One last slow song to dance to."

Stitch and Tamara danced until the song's tempo sped up. She kissed him on the cheek and then full on the lips. "Be careful!" She said!

Stitch stood shocked. "You betcha'!" was all he could think to reply.

When Stitch finished saying good-bye to his friends, he looked around for Jared but was intercepted by his father, Leon. "Come with me." Leon said. "We need to talk about a few things."

Stitch followed his father, who led him to the Airport bar. "Two Long Island Iced Teas." Leon said to the Bar Tender. Leon then turned to Stitch and told him how he regretted never having a drink with his son. The bar tender brought the tall glasses of alcohol over to the two LeRue men who drank them down quicker than they were made. Leon signaled for two more. After each of them had three drinks, Leon leaned in to share some fatherly advice with his son. "Listen to me, son. This is important." Leon took his glass and held it up; gesturing for Stitch to do that same thing. "You're not going to be in Cohoes anymore. You're going to meet a lot different people from a lot of different places. Don't judge a man before you get to know him. When it comes to people, you need to be color blind!"

"Color blind?" Stitch asked with his speech slurred and eyes drooping. "Wha' da hell er you tawkin' about, dad?"

Stitch didn't quite understand what his father was talking about, but he guessed it had something to do with racism or something like that. Stitch held up his glass in a mock toast and announced, "To being color blind!" Leon lifted his glass and tipped it to his son's. "To being color blind!"

This would be a wonderful image to keep in one's mind; a father and son toasting over their first drink as men. But it didn't end there. Leon had Stitch toasting to ten or more words of wisdom and three more glasses of Long Island Iced Teas. By the time Stitch got on the plane bound for Boot Camp, he was stinking drunk! Either Leon didn't realize how much of a lightweight his son was, or it was his plan all along.

As the recruits were all called to their gates, Melanie stopped Stitch and presented him with a necklace she made for him. It was a green length of yarn, tied into a circle. It had a red heart, made of construction paper, and glued to it was her school picture. "I made this for you so you won't forget about me."

Stitch knelt down, cleared his drunken haze long enough to hug his sister and reassure her that he could never forget someone so special to him. He gave her a hug and kissed her head and said goodbye one last time to his family as he staggered towards the gate that would take the young boy away from Cohoes.

While on the plane, a flight attendant passed by Stitch and asked if anyone would like a drink. Stitch, already half-cocked and feeling more like a man than he really was, instructed the attractive woman to bring him a Dry Martini. Although Stitch had no idea what a dry martini was, he'd heard that drink mentioned on a movie and wanted to see what the big fuss was about. Once he got the drink, he wasn't too sure he'd ever be drinking one of them ever again. Little did he realize that he'd just made matters worse for himself. By the time the plane landed, Stitch was feeling more and more like vomiting.

The recruits disembarked the plane at O'Hare Airport where they were instructed to gather up in one specific spot. However, Stitch was not feeling very well so he layed on the floor at Jared's feet. Literally.

"Hey, man. Are you okay?" Jared asked, worried that Stitch would *yak* right in the middle of the airport.

"I'm good for now." Stitch replied. He let his face and hands and chest absorb the cool feeling of the marble floor in the airport's main lobby area. Stitch used the sheet, with the good-bye message from his friends, as a pillow, after he rolled and folded it up. He remained curled up on the floor, hoping the horrible feeling would pass. He'd only had one hangover in his life and that was the time he drank wine with his mother and Aunt Percy at a Christmas party. He had felt so sick and unable to move that he just wanted to die. It seemed like the horrible feeling would never go away even though it had only been three hours since his drink with his father, and only two hours since he gulped down that martini. Regardless, it was two hours longer than he'd wanted to be feeling like that. Just as Stitch was getting comfortable and content with his situation, he heard a scream...

"All right, you squirming maggots!" Stitch didn't know what to think, but all he knew was someone was interrupting his rest. He put his hands over his ears and tried to block them out. "Git yer gear and git yer asses through those double doors and onto the bus that's parked outside!"

As his fellow recruits ran off to do as they were told, Stitch remained laying on the floor of the airport with his hands over his ears. The Navy Petty Officer stopped when he noticed Stitch and was quite surprised by the image of the young man curled up in a ball on the floor. He knew the young man was more than likely drunk and he decided to speak a language Stitch could understand. He approached him slowly and cautiously and got down on his hands and knees as he leaned close to Stitch's ear and screamed, "I SAID MOVE IT, MAGGOT!!!"

Stitch jumped up as if he was just electrocuted. He noticed his group making their way through a set of double doors and he quickly grabbed up his pack and his makeshift pillow and ran to catch up with his group.

Needless to say, Boot camp turned out to be exactly what Stitch needed. Other than the classes and schoolwork, it really wasn't that much more difficult than growing up in the LeRue household. There were times when his company would return to the barracks and would find all their clothes scattered all over the floors. The Company Commander, or "CC", would announce that a "white tornado" came through an open window and flung all the clothes out of the lockers. This didn't even phase Stitch, as his mother would sometimes do this to Stitch and his siblings to get them to clean up their rooms.

The CC reminded Stitch of his own father. He was tall and lanky, the way Leon was. He didn't have jet-black hair, but he had the same hands as Leon. They were rough hands with calluses and large, bluish veins that protruded from under this skin. He'd yell at everyone, all the time. Where most recruits thought they were gonna crack from all the mental abuse, Stitch was wondering what all the crying was about! His bunk was situated across from Jared's and when the CC would march up and down the barracks, yelling at everyone else, Stitch and Jared would make funny faces at one another, trying to get the other to laugh out loud and get yelled at. One time, Jared made a face that Stitch couldn't get away from and he found himself laughing out loud. He soon found the Company Commander standing nose to nose with him, screaming and yelling and Stitch couldn't help keep the laugh in. It seemed the harder he tried to hold it back, the more forceful it came out. In his mind, he wasn't face to face with a military man. He was face-to-face with Leon and Jared represented Gerti, who stood back and laughed when her son would be silly.

By the end of boot camp, it was announced that Jared's grades were not up to par and he would have to be held back with the next graduating class. Stitch was on his way out to his Advanced Training School the next day so he snuck up to the barracks where Jared was now staying. He made sure that Jared's new CC was not around when he sought Jared out and found him, sitting on the floor near his bunk, shining his Boon Dockers.

"Hey," Stitch said. "Put some pants on, man!" Jared was sitting in his boxers and t-shirt when Stitch showed up.

"What are you doing up here, man?" Jared asked as he tossed his boots to the floor. "Our Master-At-Arms is a dick-head, don't let him see you."

"I needed to say good-bye, before I left." Stitch confessed. He knew it sounded totally gay, but it was true. The two of them had been together for more than thirteen years and now they were going to be separated. "Are you okay? Do you need anything?" Stitch asked.

Jared smiled. "Nah, man; it's cool."

Stitch stood there for a moment. He wanted to hug his friend and wish him well, but he knew how much Jared would get razzed by his new company. Instead, he reached out and patted his hand on Jared's shoulder. "Keep in touch, man!"

"You too." Jared said.

As Stitch walked away, he couldn't help but feel guilty about everything. He wanted to hug his friend, he wanted to let him know what he meant to him, but instead he just walked off with a pat on the shoulder. When Stitch arrived at the end of the barracks, he stopped and looked back. Jared was still standing by his rack watching his friend go. The two of them gave an uncomfortable smile and a small wave before Stitch disappeared down the stairwell.

The next morning, Stitch boarded a bus that took him to the airport where he left for Advance Training School in Meridian Mississippi; he would learn to operate the ship's stores and would become a Ship Serviceman. However, he'd only heard from Jared on four separate occasions in the next four years. On the other hand, he'd only tried to get in touch with Jared just three of those times. Stitch finished school and received orders to a ship in San Diego while Jared eventually graduated with his new company and finished his Advance Training as an Aviation Boatswain's Mate where he went on to work as a catapult operator for the jets on aircraft carriers. Stitch was glad that at least one of them got the air craft carrier. Stitch, on the other hand, was able to visit Japan and Korea during his time on the West Coast.

Stitch eventually understood his father's words about being colored blind and blended in well with everyone on his ship. It was quite a contrast to the type of person he was in school. No longer was he was shy and reclusive. In the Navy, he was outspoken and often referred to as 'the funny guy'. But in a way, Stitch missed that little, skinny, longhaired kid from Cohoes, New York. Despite the life he complained of and hardships that he grew up with, he became thankful for them.

Growing up in a home that didn't give a lot, in the way of material things, allowed Stitch to be appreciative of the things that he was able to obtain on his own. In the Navy, he didn't have to share his bed with his brother, although he shared his living space with two hundred and eighty other men, he had a 3x6x3 foot space that was all his. He was able to close the curtains to his rack and it was like he was in his own private place. He didn't have to worry about his brother coming in and waking him up, or his sister Caitlin making noise next door when he was trying to do his homework. When shipmates complained about the ship's food, or the long work schedule, Stitch didn't mind, especially not after growing up in Leon's house! Although Leon wasn't in the Army very long, he still who ran his kids like the military. He was strong when he needed to be strong, but soft when warranted. When the ship was at sea and the regular milk went bad, the crew was forced to drink a type of soymilk that did not require refrigeration. Everyone bitched and moaned about how horrible the soymilk was. However, for Stitch, soymilk was great compared to the powdered milk he grew up drinking. Navy life was good for Stitch, but that's another story...

"Continental Flight 2983 for Cleveland is now boarding..." Stitch heard this message over the internal speaker system and was immediately pulled out of his memory. He stood up and took a last look at the place, as if he were never going to return again and then picked up his bag and headed through the gate.

Once on board, the usual scenario played out with the flight attendants giving their speeches and everyone on the plane getting comfortable and adjusted to their seats. After a few minutes of waiting, the large jet finally started pulling away from the terminal and began its taxi run up the tarmac where it placed itself in line for take off.

As Stitch's plane ascended into the skies over the Capital District of New York, Stitch leaned into the window and looked down at the lay of the land. He found the Mohawk River and with his finger on the window glass, he traced the river up the point of the Cohoes waterfalls and smiled down upon that small section, as he gave a tiny wave; not realizing that in the backyard of number four Cataract street, Marge was outside, picking up her nephew's bike and sweeping the dead leaves from the slate walk when she just happened to look up and spot a jet overheard; immediately she thought of her new friend, Stitch, who grew up in her apartment and shared a part of his life with her. Not even realizing it was, in fact, his plane; she gave a wave as a way of saying she was thinking about her new friend.

<u>END BOOK ONE</u>: Yes Yvonne - *There will be more than ONE book*

Breinigsville, PA USA
02 December 2009

228447BV00002B/6/P

9 781449 031336